"I want to feel my

"The baby can't be felt yet," Meg told him.

"But you said there was a bulge."

"It's tiny, Andy. I'm probably the only one who'd notice. It's not something you can feel through my clothes."

Andy's next suggestion was apparent by the look in his eyes.

Meg's cheeks grew warm. "Andy!"

"Well, it's not as if I haven't seen you without your clothes before. We were married, remember?"

"Well, you won't see me without my clothes again."

"But I want to see the baby growing, Meg."

"I don't think it's something I can hide, Andy. And besides, taking my clothes off was what got me in this situation in the first place!"

Dear Reader,

Welcome to Silhouette **Special Edition** . . . welcome to romance. Each month, Silhouette **Special Edition** publishes six novels with you in mind—stories of love and life, tales that you can identify with—romance with that little "something special" added in.

November brings plenty to be joyful and thankful for—at least for Andy and Meg in *Baby, It's You* by Celeste Hamilton. For with the birth of their child, they discover the rebirth of their love . . . for all time. Don't miss this compelling tale!

Rounding out November are more dynamite stories by some of your favorite authors: Bevlyn Marshall (fun follows when an abominable snowman is on the loose!), Andrea Edwards, Kayla Daniels, Marie Ferrarella and Lorraine Carroll (with her second book!). A good time will be had by all this holiday month!

In each Silhouette **Special Edition** novel, we're dedicated to bringing you the romances that you dream about—the type of stories that delight as well as bring a tear to the eye. And that's what Silhouette **Special Edition** is all about—special books by special authors for special readers!

I hope you enjoy this book and all of the stories to come.

Sincerely,

Tara Gavin
Senior Editor

CELESTE HAMILTON
Baby, It's You

Silhouette Special Edition

Published by Silhouette Books New York

America's Publisher of Contemporary Romance

For Jessica Ann & Dylan Joseph,
the newest Hamiltons.
You may be Jeff and Donna's miracles,
but you own a big piece of your aunt's heart.

SILHOUETTE BOOKS
300 East 42nd St., New York, N.Y. 10017

BABY, IT'S YOU

ISBN: 0-373-09708-5

First Silhouette Books printing November 1991

Printed in the U.S.A.

Books by Celeste Hamilton

Silhouette Special Edition

Torn Asunder #418
Silent Partner #447
A Fine Spring Rain #503
Face Value #532
No Place To Hide #620
Don't Look Back #690
Baby, It's You #708

Silhouette Desire

*The Diamond's Sparkle #537
*Ruby Fire #549
*The Hidden Pearl #561

*Aunt Eugenia's Treasures

CELESTE HAMILTON

has been writing since she was ten years old, with the encouragement of parents who told her she could do anything she set out to do and teachers who helped her refine her talents.

The broadcast media captured her interest in high school, and she graduated from the University of Tennessee with a B.S. in Communications. From there, she began writing and producing commercials at a Chattanooga, Tennessee, radio station.

Celeste began writing romances in 1985 and now works at her craft full-time. Married to a policeman, she likes nothing better than spending time at home with him and their two much-loved cats, although she and her husband also enjoy traveling when their busy schedules permit. Wherever they go, however, "It's always nice to come home to East Tennessee—one of the most beautiful corners of the world."

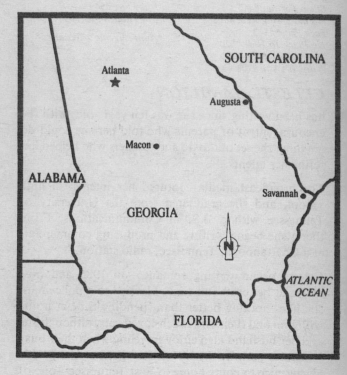

Chapter One

"Dating your ex-husband is an unhealthy habit, Meg."

In a mirrored panel on the open closet door, Meg Hathaway caught her best friend's disapproving glance. But instead of responding, she continued to rifle through the closet's untidy contents. "God, Perri, haven't you ever cleaned this out? There are clothes you haven't worn since college in here."

Perri Wheaton shifted the fretting baby she held from one arm to the other. "I have three children under the age of six. Closets are not high on my priority list."

"You need a maid."

"And you need to have your head examined. Why are you going out with Andy? Didn't we decide it was bad for you?"

Though Meg usually granted her childhood friend the privilege of interfering in her life, this was one subject she didn't want to discuss. At least not now. If she listened, Perri might begin making sense. Meg didn't want to be sensible. Not tonight, anyway.

"Here's what I was looking for," she cried, dragging a black dress from its cushioned hanger. A row of rhinestones glittered as she held the dress against her and turned from the closet. "Lucky this is knit. It doesn't matter that you crushed it into the closet. Do you think it will look okay on me?"

Her expression glum, Perri sank down onto the edge of the bed and lifted the baby to her shoulder. "I think you've suffered a temporary mental lapse brought on by your thirty-second birthday."

"Oh, stop it," Meg said, finally acknowledging Perri's disapproval. "Andy and I are just going to dinner."

"And you're *just* going to wear the sexiest dress in my prepregnancy wardrobe."

Meg tossed the dress over a nearby chair and began unbuttoning her blouse. "That's only because I got tied up at the office, and I didn't have time to get to my place, change and get back downtown to meet Andy." Perri still looked skeptical, but Meg wasn't about to admit she had been thinking of nothing but this sexy dress ever since Andy called. "You know Atlanta traffic on Friday afternoons," she improvised. "It really was quicker for me to come over here than to go home."

"You could wear what you have on."

"But it's my birthday," Meg said as she stepped out of her black skirt. "I want to look nice."

Patting the baby on the back with one hand, Perri used the other to indicate her loose T-shirt. A myriad of stains, ranging from milk seepage to finger paints, decorated the front. "At this moment, your little black suit looks pretty nice to me. Wanna change places?"

"As if you would." Meg went to the mirror and tugged the dress over her head. She settled the clingy knit into place and ran a hand through her ebony hair, continuing, "You know you're exactly where you want to be, Perri." But when her friend was silent, she turned back around. "You are happy, aren't you? I know you and Rod didn't count on having a third baby, but you've resolved all that, haven't you?"

The baby responded for Perri, with a loud, most unladylike burp. The two women shared a startled glance, then burst into giggles.

Meg sat on the bed and lightly touched the baby's downy hair, which was as fiery red as Perri's. She was so tiny, so in need of the shelter Perri's arms offered. "Is she all right?" Meg asked as the baby whimpered and burped again, softer this time.

Green eyes bright with amusement, Perri laughed. "She's fine. Unlike her mom or her Aunt Meg, little Jocelyn has a very simple life. She eats and burps and wets her diaper and then sleeps and eats and wets and burps some more. After just one month, she has no complications, no regrets, no ex-husbands to call her up every birthday and upset her life...."

Muttering about one-track minds, Meg went to the dresser and began brushing her shoulder-length page-boy into place. "I'm not upset."

"And how will you feel in the morning?"

The quiet question brought a muffled exclamation from Meg. "You'd think after all these years I'd learn not to tell you everything. Just because Andy and I—well, you know—got intimate a couple of years ago on my birthday..."

"I thought it was last year."

Meg flushed, reluctantly meeting Perri's gaze. "So it was last year."

"And a couple of years before that?"

"Perri—"

"In the eight years since you guys split up, I'll bet you've—"

"So I gave in to temptation a couple of times," Meg interrupted. "Was it a crime? I mean, it always happened when Andy wasn't dating anyone and neither was I. It wasn't as if we were being unfaithful to anyone or promiscuous or anything. We have a history together. Things got out of control."

Perri cocked an eyebrow. "*Things*—as you so delicately call sex—have been out of control between the two of you from the beginning."

The beginning. Meg pretended concern over the dress's hem while she thought back to the day she had met Andy. Meg could see Andy as he had looked nearly ten years ago, with his mussed dark honey hair and deep blue eyes, stepping into her apartment to investigate a burglary. He'd had a cocky grin and a rookie cop's swagger in his walk. Of course the swagger had nothing to do with being a cop. It was just Andy. Reckless, passionate Andy. He was the only man who had ever induced her to take chances. She had married him two months after that first meeting.

"Oh, good grief."

Perri's groan brought Meg back to the present. "What is it?"

"I don't like that look in your eyes."

"What look?"

"That I'm-going-to-see-Andy-so-I'm-melting look."

Meg stiffened her shoulders. "I never melt. Whatever I do is what I *choose* to do. Ask all my clients. Even IRS audits don't make me wilt."

Shaking her head, Perri stood. "Honey, the IRS is nothing next to the heat you and Andy generate when you're together."

The heat. Yes, there was something hot between her and Andy. Meg shivered just thinking abouut it. It was a pity great sex hadn't been enough to hold a marriage together.

"I wonder," Perri mused. "Has Andy grown up enough to give marriage another shot?"

"Andy will never be ready for marriage."

"You're right. Emotionally unavailable men, however sexy they might be, rarely change. And there are women—like yourself—who continue to be attracted to them.''

Meg looked at Perri in amazement, then laughed. ''You've been watching too many talk shows with too many pop psychologists as guests, my friend.''

''No,'' Perri said, all trace of teasing gone from her voice and expression. ''I've spent too many years watching you ride the Andy Baskin roller coaster. He calls you or you call him, you see each other and this…this *thing* between you explodes. You feel guilty and avoid him for a few weeks until he stops calling. Then, eventually, one of you starts it all over again.'' She sighed. ''Meanwhile, you don't take any other man seriously. For years you've avoided getting on with your life. If you're in love with Andy—''

''We established long ago that I didn't love Andy,'' Meg retorted. ''I find him exciting and intriguing, but do I love him? No.''

''Then why aren't you going out with someone else tonight?''

Meg forced a light tone into her voice. ''Don't you know, Perri, you got the last decent man.''

At that moment, a chorus of ''Daddy's home!'' came from the family room where Perri's four- and five-year-old boys had been watching television. Perri grinned. ''You could stay here tonight. Three of the last decent guys in the world are here and would love to help you blow out some candles.'' She nodded toward the bedside telephone. ''Why don't you call Andy and cancel?''

Meg considered the possibility while Perri went to greet her husband. Perhaps her friend was right. Perhaps meeting Andy would only perpetuate some destructive cycle she had begun years ago. It was just that seeing Andy always made Meg feel so alive, so...female. Though she had been involved with other men, no one affected her quite like Andy. And today, on her birthday, she wanted to feel that way. She needed a lift.

Sighing, Meg pulled a cosmetics bag from her purse and began freshening her makeup. She certainly wasn't silly enough to consider herself old at the age of thirty-two. Except when she thought of Perri and her three kids. Meg paused, amazed as always by the fact that she and Perri had chosen such different paths and managed to remain friends. Happy-go-lucky, disorganized Perri had *three* children. While Meg had none.

She set aside her lipstick and listened to the cacophony of family sounds coming from the other end of the house. For a second she gave in to the envy that sometimes crawled through her when she saw what Perri had. If she and Andy had stayed together...

"No," she said aloud. Her dark eyes narrowed as she stared at her reflection. "You're not going to play the what-if-I-had-stayed-with-Andy game." Years ago, when she and Andy were together, Meg hadn't wanted diapers and mortgage payments and a minivan in the driveway. She had wanted exactly what she had—a briefcase, a condo and a BMW. Perri had realized her dreams. Meg had found hers, too.

So why did Meg feel like crying?

"Don't be stupid," she instructed herself, blinking away the tears. Again she considered calling Andy. Then she squared her shoulders. Meg Hathaway met challenges head-on. And tonight's challenge was seeing Andy and not giving in to the sexual temptation he always presented to her. She was a grown-up and, as Perri had pointed out, it was time she got on with her life. Tonight was going to be the beginning. She was getting off the Andy Baskin roller coaster.

But half an hour later, across a crowded room, Meg's gaze met Andy's, and she felt herself sliding down the first dip in a never-ending ride.

Why did I let this woman go?

The question, which had presented itself many times in the past eight years, was renewed as Andy watched Meg thread her way through the smoky restaurant lounge where he leaned against the bar. Their gazes clung, while the usual regrets, mixed with desire, pressed through him. He had wanted Meg from the first moment they met. Even now, what he'd like was to find a place where he could touch her face, kiss her mouth and move his hands up the creamy skin of the long, elegant legs revealed by her dress's abbreviated skirt. Andy was intimately acquainted with every inch of those legs. Indeed some of his fondest memories were the times those legs . . .

"Andy?"

Meg's voice brought him back from the no-man's-land of remembered and now-forbidden delights. Setting down his beer, he took her hand. Her dark eyes widened, and he felt her slight shiver. It was the same old chemistry, the attraction he kept telling himself would someday disappear.

Dropping her hand, he summoned a grin. "Happy birthday, Meggy."

Her laughter was nervous. "You're still the only person who calls me that."

"Good."

His gruff, almost proprietary tone brought a silence between them, an intensity in the atmosphere that made Meg glance away and Andy clear his throat and reach for his beer. "Our table should be ready soon. As you can see, there's no place to sit in here. But I can get you a drink."

Her dark-as-midnight hair brushed her shoulders as she shook her head. Andy followed the movement of the silky tendrils with something akin to hunger growing inside. He took another swig of beer.

Meg let out a breath and said, "You look great, Andy."

"So do you." Though he knew he shouldn't, Andy let his glance sweep over her again, taking in the sparkling buttons and the clinging fabric that emphasized Meg's slender curves. He cleared his throat once more. "I like the dress. It's not your usual—"

"Style," she completed for him, grinning. "I borrowed it from Perri. I felt adventurous..." She broke off, frowning, as if annoyed at her words.

Andy tried not to smile. So she felt *adventurous*. Years ago, that word had been their secret password in case one of them wanted to leave a party or dinner with friends, a signal that one of them was feeling sexy.

"I didn't mean it that way," Meg said, following Andy's train of thought. "I meant, it's my birthday and I wanted to wear something different."

"Of course," Andy agreed, this time hiding his smile by draining his mug. "And you do look different. I like it."

Meg looked as if she were about to protest his compliment when the hostess arrived to escort them to their table. Following Meg through the restaurant, Andy tried his best not to focus on the gentle sway of her hips. The dress really wasn't her usual, subtle choice, but on her even a football jersey would have looked elegant. Meg had always presented a polished facade to the world. The years had added more sophistication. There was a sleekness about her—from the top of her smooth dark hair to the tips of her slender feet.

Andy touched the faint stubble on his chin and adjusted the lapel of his gray summer tweed jacket, wishing he'd had time to go home and change. At least the restaurant looked like the kind of place where Meg belonged. Not too trendy. Not pretentious, either. Muted lighting and music. The sweet smell of potted flowers mingling with spices in the air. Well-spaced tables and carved wooden partitions ensured some privacy, especially at the small corner table where Meg and Andy were seated.

"This looks wonderful," Meg said after the hostess had left them with the menus.

Andy was pleased. "One of the detectives recommended the place. She said it was French, but the food was like, you know...*real* food, not one of those places where they put a piece of fish and a couple of spears of asparagus on a plate and call it dinner."

Having taken him to *those* sort of places in the past, Meg smiled. So did Andy. And some of the tension between them ebbed. The waiter took their order, brought wine, and Meg began to think she could follow through on her resolve to resist her ex-husband's magnetism.

What made him so appealing? It wasn't that Andy was truly handsome, Meg decided while savoring the delicate flavor of her favorite chardonnay. Andy was of average height, with a wiry build that wasn't as muscular as current Schwarzenegger-inspired male perfection was defined. His face was a little too long, his hair a little too shaggy around the edges. But his smile was broad and easy. When his amusement was genuine, his eyes crinkled at the corners and their blue depths sparkled. His smile was what had drawn her from the start. That teasing, wheedling grin had often made her lose her head.

As he smiled at her now, Meg sat back in her chair. The table, which only a moment ago put a safe distance between them, now seemed all too small.

"How's the job?" she asked, deliberately choosing a subject that had divided them in the past.

"The usual murder and mayhem," Andy said, his tone light.

She struggled to hold on to her smile. "You're still working homicide?"

"For now. There's a new task force on narcotics being formed. I'm thinking about requesting a change."

The thought sent a cold chill spiraling through Meg. In Atlanta's urban sprawl, drugs were the police's most potent enemy. A new initiative in the battle against them would be the right place for someone like Andy—a leader, an officer who was always the first through the door. She tried to keep her voice from mirroring her all-too-familiar fears for him. "That would be more dangerous, wouldn't it?"

"Perhaps." Andy took a sip of his wine and then smiled teasingly again. "The people I deal with now are mostly already dead. They don't shoot at me much."

Meg glared at him. "I'll never understand how you can laugh about what you do."

"Don't you laugh about some of the stuffed shirts you have to rescue from taxpayer's hell?"

"Sure, but—"

"It's the same with me."

She shook her head. "But it's life and death."

"It's my job."

"Andy—"

"Please," he interrupted, his voice frosty. "Could we not argue about something we're never going to agree on?"

Only then did Meg realize she had leaned forward, straining toward him as if in battle. Challenging Andy about his job was no longer her right or her duty. She eased back in her seat. There was no hint of amusement in the steady blue eyes that gazed at her now. She had succeeded in destroying the sexually charged atmosphere that had enveloped them from the moment they had seen each other. Andy's job and the screen of humor he used to disguise his true feelings about it had always come between them.

And always would.

"I'm sorry," she said softly. "Arguing with you wasn't my intention tonight."

"Mine, either." His shoulders relaxed.

Meg forced herself to say, "I'm glad you're happy with your job." Andy's gaze sharpened again, and she hurried to add, "Truly, I am. Being happy with your job is one of the most important things in the world."

He drained his wine and glanced away. "To some people a job's just a job."

"Who do you know like that?" she asked without giving the question any thought. She expected he would lie and say himself. It would be like Andy to say he hated what meant the most to him.

But Andy surprised her. "Every day for over thirty-five years, my father has gone down to the plant, done his job, come home and forgotten it till the next morning."

Meg could believe that of Andy's stern, remote father. During the year and a half she and Andy had been married, she didn't think she had ever heard genuine laughter from the man. Perhaps that was why Andy's mother had laughed too much. There were secrets in that family, pain too deep to be touched. But his family was another subject she and Andy had never been able to explore. And Meg wasn't going in search of another argument now.

"Sometimes I wish I could forget the office," she commented lightly. "It seems I'm always bringing it home with me."

"Has Parrish, Bailey and Smythe Financial Services made you a vice president yet?"

Meg chose to ignore the slight sarcasm she detected in Andy's tone. "I'm sure it will happen in the next year or so. My clients are pleased with the work I do for them."

"I'm sure they are." Now there was no ignoring the twist Andy's derisive smile put on his words.

"And what do you mean by that?" Meg demanded. She had forgotten how Andy could make her dedication to her career seem like a less-than-desirable trait.

Andy pushed his empty wineglass away. "I only meant that I'm sure your clients are crazy about you."

"Any reason why they shouldn't be?"

"God, Meg, you take everything—"

"Excuse me." The waiter's appearance with their salads forestalled further conversation. After he departed, they ate in silence, a condition that lasted well into the main course.

Meg finally pushed her plate away. "Well, what do you want to talk about now, Andy? I mean, we've touched on almost all the taboo subjects."

Andy nodded grimly. "My job."

"And mine."

"Even my family."

"Should we go for broke and talk about my family or should we jump right into some of the big stuff—like money and sex?"

"Sex was never a problem," Andy reminded her.

She looked away, thinking how only a short while before she had been wondering how to stay out of bed with this man. "Maybe that makes sex the biggest problem of all."

Andy set his fork down. Reaching across the table, he took Meg's hand. "What are we doing?" he asked, his voice deepening.

She glanced up, surprised by the degree of despair she heard in his tone and saw in his face. "We're making a mistake," she said, after a moment or two of silence. "I shouldn't have come tonight."

"That's not what I mean."

"But we keep doing this over and over again," Meg insisted, thinking of what Perri had said earlier. "And what we *should* do is not see each other at all. Then we wouldn't fight. We wouldn't be..." Her voice faltered and she tugged her hand from his grasp.

"Then we wouldn't be tempted?"

"Exactly."

He gave a short laugh. "Two grown-ups should be able to keep their emotions under control, shouldn't they?"

"That's exactly what I promised myself I was going to do tonight."

"Then let's do it."

Meg smiled at the resolve in his voice. "As we have proven too many times, it's not so easy."

"It is if we don't follow our usual pattern."

"What's that?"

He ticked the items off on his fingers. "First, we try to hide our attraction to each other. Second, we try to avoid the attraction by arguing about anything and everything we ever disagreed about. That's when the emotions start to really roil. And then third, we wind up in bed, exhausting those emotions and trying to act as if it were all an accident."

Meg flushed. "We sound like idiots."

"Not idiots. Human beings." He reached for her hand again. "Human beings who happen to have the hots for each other."

Glancing at their joined hands, Meg felt her face grow even warmer. She looked at Andy and found color spreading across his cheeks, also. Slowly, their gazes not faltering, they both pulled their hands away.

"Okay," Andy murmured. "We've admitted our attraction. We're not dancing around it. We're not denying it. We're facing the problem. That's the first step in beating it."

"You talk like we're addicts."

"Maybe we are." He leaned forward again, moistened his lips as if in preparation to speak, then closed his mouth.

"What?" Meg prompted.

Nervously he rubbed a hand along his jaw. "I want to be completely honest, Meg, okay? I just want you to know that those times when we've...um...when we've given in to temptation...I didn't take them lightly."

Meg's voice dropped to match his. "I know that."

Now his gaze didn't quite meet hers. "You're special, Meg. I loved you once. And I guess I'll have the hots for you for forever." He looked at her, his blue eyes so dark they were almost black. "There are days when I wish we could have made it."

"Me, too," she admitted, her voice catching.

"But we can't."

"We're too different."

"We've always been too different. And we're not likely to change. Not at our age."

"No. People don't change." Even as she spoke the words, Meg knew they weren't completely true. For she had changed in the past eight years. She wasn't the same rigid young feminist who had scornfully refused to add her husband's name to her own, who had cringed at the thought of babies and houses in the suburbs, who said compromising her ideals wasn't part of her value system. Now, as she sat with Andy, Meg admitted what she had only partially faced earlier at Perri's. She wanted some of the traditional predictability her best friend had found.

But she would never find it with Andy.

Meg didn't know why that knowledge hit her like a
blow to the gut. She had realized long ago she and
Andy would never have anything more than fantastic
sex. But there was a part of her, a place deep in her
heart, that had always harbored some hope of resur-
recting their dead relationship. She had been denying
that hope for years even as she acted out these little
flirtations with Andy. And today, faced with the pas-
sage of one more year of her life, when she finally began admitting some of her secret yearnings for a
family, that hope had brought her straight to Andy.
Only Andy wasn't her destiny. He was leftover business, something she needed to finish before she could
go on.

"Birthdays, hormones and memories," she whispered.

Andy blinked. "What?"

She stared at him, feeling as if someone had just
clubbed her with a bat. "I think I'm beginning to understand myself. And you."

"Then clue me in," Andy said, his voice full of
yearning. "I'd sort of like to know who I am."

Such an introspective question, however broad,
wasn't something she usually expected from him.
"Why, Andy, I always thought that was one question
you could answer without hesitation."

"Just one more thing you never knew about me, I
guess."

His sadness was troubling. Meg's brows drew together as she studied him. "There are some things I do

know," she said finally, because he seemed to expect some sort of reply from her. "I know you're strong, brave, loyal—"

"I sound like the perfect pet."

She smiled. "Just the perfect ex-husband. And friend."

"Friends," Andy echoed, summoning a poor imitation of his usual cocky grin. "Friendship is what we need to concentrate on, isn't it?"

Meg knew that if this was your average television sitcom, she and Andy would now shake hands, share a misty-eyed smile and the credits would roll over their faces. Today would make a fine episode of a program called, for instance, *The Life and Times of Meg Hathaway*. Next week she'd have another guest, another crisis to solve.

But life wasn't a sitcom.

Emotions, especially those she and this man had shared over the years, weren't so easy to define or change.

And just looking at Andy made her ache. All of the conclusions she had reached about herself and what she wanted from life became cloudy and uncertain when she gazed into his eyes.

So instead of shaking hands, they sat stiffly at the table, finishing a meal that had grown cold, talking about unimportant people and things, ordering coffee and a fattening dessert to celebrate her birthday. The chocolate could have been ashes for all Meg cared. Their voices reminded her of bells made of cheap brass: the sound wasn't pure. And as they walked through the warm May evening to the parking garage, Meg's limbs felt heavy.

Dread, she decided. It was dread she was feeling. Dread, because, if she was smart, there would never be another day when she'd race around with excitement because she was going to meet Andy. This was the way she should have felt eight years ago. But she didn't remember there being this much pain.

They came to a stop beside her car. Leaning against the driver's door, Meg stared at Andy, wondering if this was the last time she'd see him.

"Well . . ." he said. It sounded like an exit line, but he made no move to go.

"Thanks for dinner."

"Happy birthday." His laugh sounded nervous. "Again."

Then he took her hand, and Meg knew, the minute he touched her, what would follow. Hand-holding was only a step away from kissing. At least that's what she told herself as she covered the two paces required to put herself in Andy's arms. Then his mouth was on hers, and she stopped telling herself anything. She simply gave herself over to the heat.

White-hot.

Out of control.

Andy was the one who ended the kiss. Holding her away, he said her name brokenly and drew her close again. Then he grew stiff, muttered an oath and thrust her aside. She would have fallen if she hadn't caught hold of her car's side mirror.

Meg's head was reeling so wildly that at first she wondered why she was screaming. It took a moment to realize the screams were coming from someone else. That's when she saw the woman and man engaged in a struggle on the other side of the garage. And Andy, good old, first-one-through-the-door Andy, was running toward them, yelling, "Police!" in his best strong, courageous and loyal voice.

Heaviness again seized Meg as she started after him. "Drop the purse!" she screamed at the woman, who seemed to have a death grip on her handbag's strap. "Let him have it!" Meg might have screamed Andy's name, too. She was never sure.

For in the next moment, the thief launched himself at Andy.

And a switchblade flashed beneath the garage's dim lights.

Chapter Two

"Well, do you feel like a hero?"

Andy eased off the examining table and looked up to find Meg standing in the doorway of the emergency room cubicle. There was a hole in her stockings over her left knee, and one of the sparkling buttons was missing from her dress, but otherwise she looked fine. Pale, with eyes wide and dark with concern, but all in one piece, thank God.

Instinctively trying to make light of the past few hours' events, he touched the bandage covering the cut on his jaw. "Only five stitches. That doesn't meet the minimum requirements for hero status." His attempt at laughter dissolved into a wince.

Meg stepped into the room. "It must hurt."

"Only a little. And think of the great scar I'll have. Women love scars."

Her mouth tightened. "It isn't funny, Andy. He could have killed you."

"Yeah, well, it's my luck this guy was whacked-out on something and decided to take out his aggression on the first available cop." For a moment, Andy saw the flash of the knife again and felt the sting of pain along his jaw. He turned away from Meg, closed his eyes and steadied himself by taking a deep breath. But what he breathed in was the peculiar odor known only to hospitals—a mix of ammonia and wilting flowers. He hated that smell and the memories it evoked.

Impatiently straightening his shoulders, he plucked his torn and bloodstained jacket from a nearby chair. "I guess I can retire this," he said, holding it up for Meg's inspection.

She took the jacket from him. "You're lucky the guy didn't know how to fight."

"He was just a punk kid."

"But he would have stuck that knife in your ribs."

"But he didn't." Andy looked at her and in his sternest tones said, "In the future, Ms. Hathaway, if you see two guys struggling over a knife, don't interfere."

"All I did was hit him with that stupid woman's purse. I don't know what she had in the thing, but it weighed a ton."

"I thought he was out cold for a minute," Andy said, momentarily amused as he remembered the wallop Meg had delivered to his assailant's head. The blow had stunned the guy enough to allow Andy to knock the knife out of his hand and subdue him. But Meg could have gotten hurt. The thought sobered him. "You took a terrible chance."

"I couldn't stand there and watch somebody kill you!"

"Nobody was going to get killed."

"I didn't know that at the time."

"But still—"

"Is this a private argument or can anyone jump in?"

Andy turned, startled by the familiar voice. "Lisa," he said to the tall blonde who had paused outside the door. "What are you doing here?"

She came into the room, her smile and nod including both Andy and Meg. "I was working late on a case when one of the officers going off duty told me you got yourself cut chasing a purse snatcher. I decided to make sure you were okay. Obviously, you survived, Lieutenant Hotshot."

"Meg beat the guy up with a purse," Andy said, grinning.

Meg made a sound between a laugh and a grunt and ignored him. "Hello, Lisa," she said, holding out her hand. "It's been a while since I've seen you."

Touching his bandaged jaw again, Andy watched the two women exchange greetings. His best friend and his ex-wife. To see them now, one would never suspect Meg had once accused him of having an affair with Lisa. Of course, the allegation had been preposterous. He and Lisa had once been partners. The bond that develops between police officers was just one more thing Meg had never understood about his job. Sometimes it was easier to talk to a fellow officer than a wife. But then, most fellow officers didn't have Lisa's traffic-stopping figure and big blue eyes. So maybe it was understandable that Meg had resented the time he had spent with her. Though he had never told Lisa about Meg's accusations, Lisa had to have known something, because Meg used to freeze the woman out every time they were together.

But at the moment, the smile Meg sent the other woman was warm. "Didn't Andy tell me you're a detective now?"

"Specializing in arson investigations."

"And how's your husband?"

Lisa cut her eyes toward Andy. "I guess Andy didn't tell you I'm divorced."

Meg didn't miss a beat. "No, he didn't."

Andy wondered just what Meg was making of that bit of omitted information. She betrayed nothing, not even glancing his way. Just as Lisa wasn't acting surprised to see him here with his ex, although he could imagine the wheels spinning in her head.

Smiling, Lisa reached for her purse. "I'm sure Andy has told you about my little boy, though. And I just happen to have a couple of dozen pictures of him."

Meg was well into gushing over the second dozen snapshots when Andy decided he had to break this up. "You know, ladies, they might need this room for people who are really hurt. Maybe we should move the party elsewhere."

Lisa grinned. "My, but we're grouchy, aren't we? The deadening in that cut must be wearing off."

"It doesn't hurt," Andy said tersely, even though the ache was spreading to his cheek. "But I think I'd like to go."

Tucking the photographs back into her purse, Lisa started toward the door. "I can take a hint. You'd better get him home, Meg. You know men and their tolerance for pain."

Andy muttered, "Obviously, my tolerance for pain-in-the-butt women is high."

Lisa waved goodbye. "Try to stay out of trouble for the rest of the night, Hotshot." And before she left the room, Andy caught the arched-brow glance she directed from him to Meg. Next time Lisa saw him, he knew he would get the third degree.

He looked at Meg, whose color was high and eyes were narrowed. "I hope present company is excepted from that pain-in-the-butt remark."

Playfully he placed a hand over his heart. "Of course. You're my hero." Once more his attempted grin ended in a wince.

Taking his arm, Meg urged him toward the door. "Come on, let's get you home."

"Just get me back to my car."

"Somebody from the force can drive you over to get it in the morning. I'll take you home. I assume the address is still the same."

Andy didn't argue with her. For one thing, his jaw *was* hurting. For another, he hadn't forgotten the kiss he and Meg had shared before the purse snatching had

brought the evening to a screeching halt. He knew it
was crazy to even think about that kiss. It had been an
accident. An old habit. One they had agreed was no
good for either of them. He should let it pass.

But letting things pass wasn't Andy's strong suit.
His dogged pursuit of conclusions was one quality that
made him a good cop. He had often turned seemingly
dead-end leads into case-opening clues. However, such
determination hadn't worked to his advantage in
dealing with Meg in the past. All too often, he had
pushed her a little too hard, a little too far. Maybe he
shouldn't push tonight. Perhaps he should sit back
and see what happened.

As she turned her expensive little gray car onto a
busy Atlanta highway, Andy half closed his eyes and
pretended to rest. In reality he studied what he could
see of Meg's profile in the dim light. She drove the way
she did most everything, with her jaw set in determination, her concentration firm. It was her single-
mindedness he both loved and hated.

He wasn't going to think about love and hate right
now. Simply looking at Meg was nice enough. His
eyelids slipped lower. The jazz on the radio was slow,
dreamy. The car smelled like Meg's light perfume, reminding him of the mornings he had awakened to this
scent and the warmth of her body cuddled with his.
The scent helped him forget violence, pain and hospitals. Content for the moment, Andy smiled.

"When did Lisa get a divorce?"

The question brought his eyes open. Memories of
tangled sheets and smooth skin fled. Shrugging, he

glanced out the window. "I don't know. A couple of years ago."

"You never mentioned it."

"I guess I didn't think too much about it. The guy was a bum, anyway."

"So you always said."

"She and the kid are better off since he split."

Meg said nothing more while she guided the car down an exit ramp. They had turned onto Andy's street before she asked, "You and Lisa still spend a lot of time together?"

Expecting criticism, Andy stiffened. "She and I are friends, Meg. Just friends."

"I know that."

He considered his next words carefully but then said them anyway. "You didn't use to understand our friendship."

"And that was silly of me." Meg pulled the car to a stop in his driveway. "I know that now. I mean, Lisa is obviously like a sister to you."

"Right."

She cut her engine. "And I was way out of line when I thought the two of you were involved."

Andy let his breath out slowly. "Well, that's good to hear. It always bothered me that you thought I'd been unfaithful to you."

"Is that why you didn't tell me she was divorced?"

He hesitated then nodded. "I didn't want you making something of nothing."

"I'm glad she's there for you," Meg said, sounding sincere. "Everyone needs good friends."

"How true."

"Yeah, well..." She ran her hands through her hair in a nervous gesture. "Thanks again for dinner. I hope your jaw's okay."

For the second time that evening she was preparing to say goodbye. But Andy didn't want to let her go. Not yet. There was still that kiss to consider. He felt the old pushing mechanism kick in. "Why don't you come in for a minute?"

"But it's after midnight. I don't think..."

"Oh, come on, a *friend* would come in."

Meg recognized the challenge in his words. They had talked about friendship at dinner. Dinner? Their meal seemed years ago. Was it only tonight she had looked into Perri's mirror and promised herself she would control this thing with Andy? Surely more than hours had passed since his lips had moved against her own. Despite her promises, she had ended up in his arms. Remembering that foolish moment, Meg tightened her fingers on the smooth leather covering the steering wheel. Would the same thing happen if she followed Andy inside his house? Was she that weak?

"Come on," he urged again. The "if you dare" was implied by his tone.

Accepting the gauntlet he tossed down, Meg pulled her keys from the ignition and opened the car door. She followed him to the house and ignored the voice inside her head that whispered a warning.

Meg had been to Andy's house several times, but as always, its homey atmosphere caught her off guard. Before they married, he had lived in a small, cluttered apartment. He had been messy during their marriage. But since buying this aging ranch house a few years back, he had proven more domestic.

She trailed Andy through the large main room, touching a leafy plant on the coffee table, pausing to look at the framed photos on a bookshelf. There was Andy in his uniform the day he graduated from the police academy. Here were his parents. And a single shot of his older brother.

Surprised, Meg picked up the framed photograph. David must have been fifteen or sixteen here—about the age he'd been when he was killed. She was sure this photo hadn't been here the last time she visited. When she and Andy were married, even talking about David had been discouraged. Maybe this picture meant Andy was dealing with some of the hurt in his past. Maybe he'd stopped trying to make up for David's death. She hoped so.

She looked up to find Andy's gaze on her. Though he glanced at the photograph, he said nothing. But then David wasn't a subject she would expect him to talk about. She carefully put the photo back in place.

"You want something to drink?" Andy asked as he moved into the dining area.

"A diet cola if you have it."

He nodded. "Let me take care of the dog first."

Meg continued looking around the room. The blue sectional sofa was new, as was the landscape hanging on the wall over Andy's ancient gray leather recliner. They had bought the chair together. There had been moments in that chair... Hugging her crossed arms to her midriff, she avoided those memories while Andy opened one of the glass-paned doors that led to the back deck. He whistled for his dog.

"Here, Boomer, come on, boy. Come on."

Boomer, a beautiful Irish setter, bounded inside, leaped on Andy, then made a beeline for Meg.

"The old boy always has been a ladies' man," Andy said, while Meg stooped to receive several of Boomer's wet doggy kisses.

She rubbed the dog's luxuriant red coat. "He never looks any older."

"I think he's actually gotten younger since I moved here. He has plenty of room to run in the backyard, and the kids next door give him all kinds of attention."

Boomer abandoned Meg's loving ministrations to follow his master through a swinging door. Meg leaned against the bar that separated the dining area from the kitchen and watched Andy fill the dog's bowls with food and water.

"You really like living here, don't you?"

"You sound surprised."

"Well, it is a family neighborhood."

"It's the kind of place I always said I wanted to live." Andy wiped his hands on a towel and looked up at her. "Remember?"

The word seemed to vibrate between them. *Remember?* Yes, Meg remembered. She could hear Andy's voice, dreaming aloud about tree-shaded streets, backyard barbecues and the family they would have together. He had been so impatient, so sure of what she doubted. Clearly she could hear her standard replies. *"Someday. When I'm ready."*

Andy was remembering those same conversations. Meg could see it in his face. But he didn't say anything. He didn't have to. They had worn out all the necessary words long ago; those angry words had helped kill their marriage.

The very air was pulsating with memories. Andy's hands clinched into fists. Meg tensed. Even Boomer seemed to sense the shift in mood. Looking up from his food bowls, he whined deep in his throat, his big, melting black eyes going from Meg to Andy and back again.

"Andy, I . . ." Meg's voice faltered. For what was it she wanted to say, anyway?

In the gesture Andy had repeated again and again this evening, he touched his jaw. This time the bandage covering his wound came loose. "Damn this thing."

"Here, let me." Meg headed into the kitchen, glad to have something other than their shared past to occupy her brain.

Andy waved her away. "It's okay, Meg, really. . . ."

"No, let me look." As gently as she could, she peeled the bandage the rest of the way from his jaw. "I think you need another . . ." The words died, blocked by her gasp. She swallowed hard as her gaze centered on the neatly repaired but still ugly cut that slashed the flesh beneath Andy's jaw from chin to just short of his ear. This was her first good look at the wound outside the dimly lighted parking garage. "No wonder the bandage is so big," she whispered, falling back a step.

"It's just a little cut."

"You said five stitches."

"So maybe it was ten."

"Andy—"

"I'm all right, Meg. I'm always all right."

He had told her those same words every night he didn't come home when she expected. When she found out he had volunteered for dangerous jobs, when he was suspended without pay for taking unnecessary chances. Yes, he was always all right. Except one night. One horrible February evening when her worst fears almost came true.

She didn't love Andy anymore. He had shut her out far too often for her love to survive. But she still feared for him. That same old suffocating fear tightened her chest. She had felt it tonight when she saw the punk's knife. She felt it now as she stared at the ugly cut on his jaw.

Andy moved away from her, striding from the kitchen and across the dining room. Heart pounding, she followed him into a bathroom that opened off the hall. He banged open the door of the medicine cabinet over the sink, sparing only a brief glare in her direction. "Don't look at me that way, Meg."

Anger was fast replacing her fear, the same anger she had been experiencing when Lisa had interrupted their argument at the hospital. "He could have killed you, Andy."

"Could have but didn't." He stared at his reflection and grunted at the bloodstain decorating his shirt. Hurriedly the shirt was tossed aside, and, seizing a roll of gauze from the cabinet, he turned his head, angling for a view of the cut.

Meg watched him, the fury twisting her insides. "You don't ever think about dying, do you?"

"A cop who thinks about dying all the time is too paralyzed to do anyone any good."

"And what good is a dead cop?"

Andy tore off a length of gauze and managed a tight laugh. "That sounds like the beginning of a great squad room joke. What's the punch line?"

She took a deep breath. If she hadn't, she was sure she would have slapped him. "I wish you'd stop joking around long enough to really talk to me."

Busy fumbling with the medical adhesive tape, Andy shook his head. "There's nothing to talk about. What was it you expected me to do tonight? Wait for that punk to hurt that woman? I'm a policeman, Meg, I'm supposed to help people in trouble."

"But that woman was stupid. Nothing in the purse could have been worth risking her life. Or yours."

"That's beside the point."

Meg knew that, but she was in no mood to be reasonable. "The point is you didn't have to go charging over there like the cavalry rushing to the rescue."

"I expected the punk to run."

"But instead he almost killed you."

With a vicious curse, Andy threw the tape dispenser. The plastic case slapped against the ceramic tile wall and shattered. Startled, Meg jumped while Andy wheeled around, shouting. "Okay, you're right. You've always been right. I'm just a dumb, macho, gung-ho cop. And someday someone's gonna blow me away or cut me into ribbons. But what does it matter to you? You won't be my widow, so why do you care so damn much?"

The air left Meg's lungs as if she had been thrown against the wall. And the pain in her chest split into a dozen pieces. With tears filling her eyes, she stumbled into the hall, tripping over Boomer, who seemed intent on blocking her path. Then she felt Andy's hands on her arms. While she tried to free herself, he pulled her back against him. His breath was warm against her neck as she twisted her head away.

"Oh, Meggy. Meggy, I'm sorry," he muttered. "I shouldn't have said that. I didn't mean to say that. Nothing's gonna happen to me. Tonight was a fluke."

Giving up the struggle, she turned and pressed her face against the warm bare flesh of his shoulder. Andy crooned soft words of comfort. She hugged him hard as she fought to control her tears. But her voice shook when she drew away. "I'm sorry, Andy. But I got so frightened and then so angry. I'm acting like an unreasonable shrew. Just like I always did."

With gentle fingers, he smoothed the hair back from her face. One arm was still curved around her, holding her close. "No, you're not."

"I mean, I know what you did tonight was reflex. It isn't in you to be cautious when someone needs your help." She drew in another breath. "But I was so scared, Andy. You always scare me to death."

"You didn't act very scared when you came to my rescue."

"I acted on instinct."

"And it's damn good you did." Andy paused. The familiar cocky grin appeared. "The whole thing was your fault, after all."

Nonplussed. she stared up at him. "My fault?"

"If you hadn't kissed me, my head wouldn't have been so fogged."

"I kissed you?"

"Yeah, and messed up my head, as usual. Otherwise, the punk never would have cut me." He gestured to the wound. "This is your fault, Meg Hathaway."

"But you kissed me," she said, though she could remember stepping into his arms.

"No, I didn't. I was being a grown-up, as we'd agreed. You were the one who kissed me."

She pushed at his chest, but he held her tighter. "Andy—"

"If I had kissed you," he murmured, his head lowering toward hers. "It would have gone more like this..."

His lips met hers and clung, and Meg made no pretense at protesting. Though careful of his injury, her arms wound around his neck. Her mouth opened, and his tongue plunged deep inside, teasing, arousing, heating her as only Andy's kiss had ever managed to do. Her breath caught in a little gasp as he broke away and trailed nibbles down her neck.

"Mmm," he murmured. "Isn't this where we were so rudely interrupted before?"

"You're . . . you're going to start bleeding again," she managed to choke out.

"I don't give a damn." His mouth captured hers again, blocking her next protest. And in one of his smooth, patented moves, he raked her dress upward and pressed her hips toward his.

His hand on her rear made Meg pull away from his kiss and attempt to resist. "We're supposed to be grown-ups, Andy. Remember?"

He growled, a low, sexy sound that played along her nerve endings just as sweetly as the touch of his lips. "I feel very grown-up," he whispered. He dragged her hand down to the fly of his pants and held it tight against him. "Don't I feel grown-up?"

In answer, Meg fumbled with the buckle of his belt.

They made it to his bedroom, a trail of discarded clothing marking the path.

Later Meg acknowledged she had several chances to get out of the situation. They had kept their heads long enough for Andy to make use of one of the condoms stored in his bedside table. At that point, she could have called the whole thing off, even if Andy protested. And after that first, frenzied burst of love-making, they came down to earth for the time it took to rebandage his wound. She could have, *should* have left then.

But Andy gave her one of his eye-crinkling, soulful smiles. He touched her cheek, kissed her deeply and asked her to stay.

So Meg stayed.

And this time, their lovemaking transcended anything else she had felt with Andy. His touch was the same as always—light and gentle, then strong and insistent—the stroke of his hands brought her close to the edge. He held her on that precipice until she lowered her body over his and accepted his thrust.

Torso and hips straining toward hers, he rocked forward, arms encircling her, face nuzzling her breasts as she began to tremble. Her legs clasped tight around his waist while she rode the wave of their mutual completion. But instead of a slow slide back to sanity, the erotic sensations intensified. Something convulsed inside her, a pull that came from deep inside her womb. The joy of the moment, the sense of completeness, forced a sob from her. Even when their physical union was broken, the mental connection held for long, long moments. Sadness replaced ecstasy as another sob built inside her.

Meg's tears touched Andy's heart. He understood why she cried. Their lovemaking had always been intense. But this . . . this was heaven. And it only underscored what they had once had and lost. Regret rose like bile in his throat. But he said nothing. Neither did she. He just held her close, feeling her trembling fade, listening as her breathing became normal and finally relaxed into the even cadence of sleep. Even though his heart ached as fiercely as his wounded jaw, he finally slept, too.

He dreamed that Meg stayed. He rolled over, smelled her perfume and snuggled into the warmth of her body.

Yet when he opened his eyes he found the dream was a lie. Her scent remained, but the bed was empty, and the warmth came from the spring sunshine that spilled through the open window and onto the tangled sheets. He came awake in time to hear the front door close.

"Damn," Andy whispered, listening to the sound echo through his house. A car's engine soon followed.

She was gone.

He stared at the ceiling until Boomer whined and nudged at his arm with a cold, wet nose. Andy pushed himself up. "Maybe it was all a dream," he said as he stroked the dog's head. A glance at the bedside table and the two discarded foil wrappers belied that wish.

"Happy birthday, Meggy," he muttered. "We had our usual little party, and a good time was had by all."

But he couldn't bring himself to smile.

Meg made it all the way to the end of Andy's street before she had to stop. She sat at the intersection for a long time, wondering what would happen if she went back to him.

"You idiot." She slammed her car into gear. How could she think of going back? Last night had proven the same old problems still separated her and Andy. Problems no amount of fabulous sex would ever solve.

She had failed, miserably, in her resolve to stay out of his bed. Her jaw tightened. It would never happen again. This time she was driving away for good.

So why was she crying?

"Damn you, Andy Baskin," she muttered, swiping at her tears. "Why do you make me wish for something lasting, something that will hold us together?"

There were no answers on the nearly deserted Saturday morning streets. But it was that wish that Meg carried in her heart for weeks.

Chapter Three

Be careful what you wish for . . .

The old saying, a favorite of her grandmother's, was drumming inside Meg's head as she waited for Andy to join her at the same restaurant where they had dined over two months before. Maybe the wish she had made after leaving Andy's house that night had been taken under serious consideration by the gods or the Fates or whoever decided such things. For it was coming true. Only Meg wasn't sure her grandmother would be especially pleased at being right this time.

Her grandmother, Kathleen Arthur, had been a strict, albeit loving, woman. Out of necessity rather than choice, she had raised Meg's mother alone and taught her to be independent and strong. Those were qualities Meg's mother *and* father had passed on to all three of their children. But at this juncture her grandmother might think Meg was carrying independence a little too far.

"Grandma Kathy, what's done is done," Meg said out loud. Then she looked around to make sure no one at nearby tables had heard her muttering to herself. In the stress of the past few weeks, she had slipped into many one-sided conversations, making for plenty of strange looks from her secretary, business associates and clients. However, this was the first time Meg could remember addressing someone who had been dead for five years. Perhaps she was losing her mind. No, she had already lost it, she corrected—on the night she spent with Andy.

Meg wiped condensation from her water glass, checked her watch and the restaurant door. She had made certain she had a clear view of the door when she was seated. She didn't want to be surprised. She checked her watch again. Andy was late, but she had been a half hour early. And right now, her nerves were stretched to the breaking point. She couldn't imagine how he might react today. She wasn't sure how she wanted him to react. They hadn't spoken since that night. *The* night, Meg thought, smiling tightly.

It was unlike Andy not to have contacted her since then. Yesterday, when she had called to invite him here today, he had seemed reluctant to come. Only after she had insisted had he agreed....

"Meg?"

Startled, she looked up and into his blue eyes. "Where...where did you come from?" she demanded.

He frowned. "The door."

"But I was watching the door."

"Looked to me as if you were staring into space. We came right—"

"We?" Meg echoed. Only then did she notice Lisa standing just behind Andy. The pretty blonde smiled but shifted uneasily from foot to foot. Meg glanced from her to Andy and then back again, saying nothing. She made no attempt to hide her distress.

Andy nervously rubbed his jaw, where Meg could see a faint pinkish scar, his souvenir from the purse snatcher's switchblade. Haltingly he explained, "Lisa and I were...uh...discussing one of her cases. I asked her to come along for lunch."

"Oh." The simple word stuck in Meg's throat. She had to clear it to continue, "Well then...hello, Lisa. I didn't expect—that is...I didn't know..."

Lisa brushed Meg's garbled greeting aside with a wave of her hand. "It's okay, Meg, I'm not staying."

"But you have to..." Andy's voice trailed off.

"Well, if you can't..."

Andy and Meg's simultaneous, contradictory exclamations made Lisa take a step backward. Her smile grew broad as her gaze swung between them. "I don't think you guys need me around." She astounded Meg with an obvious, conspiratorial wink, and, ignoring Andy's protest, she made her way through the restaurant.

There goes my control mechanism, Andy thought, watching her leave. Dammit, she had promised to stick around, to keep him from losing his head. He had promised himself there would be no more fun and games with Meg—ever. The aftermath hurt too much. He had held tight to that promise for the past couple of months, even when his mind strayed to Meg, even when his hand went to the phone. He had instructed Lisa to help him, but now, at the first real test of his strength, she deserted him. And what had that wink been all about, anyway?

"I thought you'd be alone."

He turned to face Meg. She had cut her hair, he noticed. It was chin length instead of shoulder sweeping, but as sleek and shiny as always. Instead of a sexy dress, today she wore a navy-and-white suit—more her usual style. But she wasn't her usual cool self. He could see that in the nervous way her hand fluttered to her throat, the way her dark eyes wouldn't quite meet his.

"Aren't you going to sit down?"

He sat. "You didn't say I should come alone."

"I just thought you would."

A waitress appeared, but Andy waved her away. Meg looked askance at his impatience, and he decided to be as direct as he could. "I'm not staying. I don't think we should see each other anymore." She started to speak, but he held up a hand to stop her. "You were right the last time we met here. We're grown-ups, and—"

"I'm pregnant, Andy."

"—we should just..." He faltered as Meg's words penetrated his brain. "You're what?"

She folded her hands on the table in front of her, then clenched them together and rocked forward a little. "I'm pregnant. I'm having a baby."

Andy swallowed hard, wondering when the lump had appeared in his throat. For long, seemingly unending moments, he stared across the table at Meg's earnest, pale face. "I'm surprised," he managed at last, not sure of what else he should say.

"So was I."

Still dumbfounded, he repeated, "A baby. You never wanted a baby."

She stiffened. "I never said never, Andy. I said later."

"I didn't believe you."

"I know."

"I'm surprised you want—"

"It isn't a question of wanting," she protested.

"So you don't want it."

"Of course I want it!" She blew out an impatient breath, then seemed to gather her poise to say quietly, "Babies have been on my mind a lot lately. I'm not old, but time is slipping away. Although I never intended...I didn't plan, didn't dream this would happen, I still want this baby. Very much."

"Oh." Andy could feel his shoulders slumping as he sat back in his chair. He felt so sad, so incredibly, unbelievably sad. *A baby. Meg's baby.*

Looking at him expectantly, she cleared her throat. "I just thought you should know."

Decent of her, he thought. It would have been harder to run into her on the street one day, to have it come as a shock. Even though he felt pretty shocked right now.

"I know you're stunned, and perhaps I should have told you earlier," Meg continued, talking fast, "but I kept thinking it was a fluke. Even when I did the home test, I was sure it was a mistake." She laughed, a nervous tinkling sound. "But it isn't a mistake."

"And what does the father think?"

She blinked. "Dad?"

"No, *the* father. Your baby's father. Is he happy?"

Meg's mouth dropped open. Color stained her cheeks.

"Well?" Andy prompted, confused by Meg's agitation. "Who is he?"

Meg slapped the table hard enough to rattle the sugar bowl. In a low, furious tone, she said, "Andrew Phillip Baskin..."

He sat up straight. "What? What did I say?"

"You jerk!"

"But I just asked the guy's name!"

She threw her napkin on the table. "But you know his name. You're him... or he... I mean, you're the one... the father!"

An angry roar, which he vaguely recognized as the rush of blood, began in his ears. "No." The protest left Andy's lips before he gave it any consideration. "I can't be. You're mistaken."

"Sorry," Meg snapped, the color in her face deepening. "But you're the only possibility, chum."

"But I couldn't . . . we didn't—"

"Yes, we did!"

"Of course we did," he corrected himself. "But we . . . um . . ." Clearly he could remember those two foil wrappers on his nightstand. He could even remember the rest of the precautionary evidence. He couldn't be mistaken. It hadn't been so long ago. And it wasn't as if he'd had any overnight guests since then. "We weren't completely stupid that night, Meg."

"I know," she replied tightly. "I trusted you to take care of it."

"I did take care of it."

"You also slipped a ten percent error through a ninety percent effective device."

"But how—"

"Oh, hell!" Impatiently she pushed herself away from the table. "I'm not going to argue with you about the hows and whys of this thing. The point is, I'm pregnant. You're the father. Telling you seemed the right thing to do."

"But Meg—"

"No more buts!" Her voice rose as she stood. "I'm having a baby. You can do whatever you want!" Snatching her purse from the chair, she turned on her heel and left Andy still sputtering at the table.

He stared after her, only then realizing most of the people at tables near him were silent and staring at him expectantly. Standing, he managed a weak smile, threw some cash on the table and took off after Meg.

The July sun, fierce even for midsummer Atlanta, beat down on his head as he sprinted along the sidewalk. Meg was preparing to cross Peachtree. "Wait a minute," he said, and caught her elbow.

She shook off his hand though she made no attempt to escape. "I'm too angry to talk to you right now."

"I'm sorry. You caught me by surprise."

Belying her assertion about talking, her words came tripping out. "I can't believe you didn't think it was your baby. Why else would I be telling you? Who else's would it be? Do you think I go jumping into bed with people all the time?"

"Hell, Meg, it's been over two months since I saw you."

"Surely it occurred to you it might be your baby."

"But it was only one night, and we took precautions."

"Didn't they tell you in health class that it only takes one time? That only abstinence is foolproof?"

Thrusting a hand through his hair, Andy stared at her. He let out a long breath. "Meg, what are we going to do?"

She pressed a hand to her stomach. "Like I told you, *I'm* having this baby. It's that simple. You had to know, of course, but I don't expect you to do anything."

Andy frowned at that. "Don't expect or don't want?"

Her gaze skittered away from his. "You shouldn't feel obligated."

An unnameable emotion began to unfurl inside Andy. "Now wait a minute—"

The pedestrian sign switched on across the street, and Meg started walking. Andy followed, protesting, "What if I want to feel obligated? What if I..." Then it hit him. With the force and subtlety of a Mack truck, the full realization of what was happening slammed into Andy's gut. In the middle of the street, he grabbed Meg's arm and twirled her around to face him.

"Meggy! Damn, Meggy!" Laughter rose inside him as he caught her in his arms. "You're having a baby, Meggy."

She struggled to free herself. "Andy, please..."

"*My* baby."

The possessive pride in his voice brought Meg up short. With typical masculine arrogance, he was taking credit for something he had only moments before been protesting couldn't be true. *His* baby. How like Andy to be so incredibly selfish. Hadn't she known this would happen? During one of the long, agonizing nights she had spent since realizing this wasn't a mistake, she had toyed with the idea of moving to another city, changing her name and never telling Andy he was a father. Fleetingly she wished she had followed that impulse. Even though that wouldn't have been fair to Andy or to the baby, she knew it might have been simpler.

Two months ago she had wished she and Andy could build something lasting together. Her wish had come true. The life growing inside her was about as real, as lasting as it came. But a baby wouldn't resolve their differences. It would only complicate what was already a complex, convoluted relationship, a relationship she should have had the strength to end a good eight years ago.

"Let me go," she told Andy as horns began to blare around them.

"But, Meg, we're having a baby."

His silly, goofy smile made Meg want to slap him. For once in his life, couldn't Andy deal with a serious situation in a serious, thoughtful manner? It was just like him to be standing in the middle of the street, blocking two lanes of traffic, laughing and acting as if they were any other happily expectant couple. He was too much, entirely too much.

"Let go of me." With a last pull, Meg got out of his grasp and dashed across the street. Impatient urban motorists in the outer lanes waited till she skimmed the curb to surge forward, but blocked Andy in the middle of traffic.

Meg gasped, certain he was going to be killed. But when no one hit him, she took advantage of his temporary delay and escaped by jogging down the sidewalk and into a nearby building. She ran down a hall, ducked into the first office she came to and stood, heart pounding, waiting for Andy to appear.

"Can I help you, miss?"

She turned to find an office full of men with briefcases and a concerned-looking receptionist.

"Uh . . . I thought this was the ladies' room," Meg improvised. That brought a few chuckles, but she ended up with a key to a real ladies' room, where she stayed until she thought Andy wouldn't be waiting. It wasn't that she thought she could hide from him forever. But she couldn't talk to him right now. Looking over her shoulder the entire way, she finally sneaked out one of the building's back exits and went to her car.

Then she drove to Perri's.

Perri was the first person Meg told when she suspected she might be pregnant. Aside from the doctor and now Andy, Perri was the *only* person who knew. Meg couldn't find the words to tell other friends or co-workers or her parents or her brother and sister that she was pregnant, especially that she was pregnant with her *ex*-husband's baby and was planning to raise the child on her own. Such behavior wasn't something people expected from someone as methodical and sensible as Meg. But Perri understood, in much the same way she had understood Meg's need to dye her hair blond in the seventh grade. She might not approve, but she understood. And, God bless her soul, this was one occasion when Perri refrained from any I-told-you-so lectures.

It was at Perri's that Meg had felt the first stirrings of joy over this baby. A few weeks ago, she had been sitting cross-legged on the floor of the nursery, bemoaning her predicament, while Perri nursed baby Jocelyn. Meg busily rattled off all the reasons why she shouldn't be having this child, but all the while, she had gazed with wonder at the tiny bit of sweetness in Perri's arms. The same sort of miracle was growing inside her. The maternal longings Meg had yet to admit to anyone else were coming to fruition.

In her usual clear-thinking fashion, Perri finally shushed Meg. "You're not fooling me, you know. I can tell you really want this baby."

And Meg had begun to cry. For Perri was right. She wanted this baby desperately. Even though she hadn't a clue as to how she would combine her demanding career with child rearing. Even though everyone else might disapprove. Yes, even though the child was Andy's, she wanted to have it.

Admitting her feelings to her best friend was a relief. During the past few weeks, Perri responded with good, straight talk about the realities of the situation.

Today was no exception. When Meg burst into the house, hot and disheveled, Perri shooed children away, cleared toys and diapers from her kitchen table and sat Meg down for a cooling glass of lemonade. She listened quietly while Meg told her about Andy's reaction to the news.

Rolling the chilled glass between her hands, Meg said, "He was so happy about it. So damn pleased with himself."

Perri studied her with a frown. "Did you really think he wouldn't care about the baby?"

"Maybe I hoped he wouldn't," Meg admitted.

"That's hardly fair. This is his baby, too."

"But the conception was an accident. And it would be simpler if he would just stay out of the way."

Fixing Meg with a steady gaze from her clear green eyes, Perri shook her head. "Andy always wanted a baby. It's one of the things you guys fought about."

"We fought about everything."

"You were both immature."

"Then we're still immature, because we still fight about everything. The aftermath of an argument is what got us into this mess."

"I think my little black dress had something to do with it."

Meg groaned and bent forward, laying her forehead against the table's cool tiled surface. "This poor baby. She has two disagreeable nincompoops for parents."

"That's not true."

"But I can see us down the road," Meg said, raising up again. "Andy and I will disagree about schools and discipline and everything."

"Aren't you getting a little ahead of yourself? You're inventing problems."

"Invention has never been necessary where Andy was concerned."

Perri got up to refill her glass. Turning from the refrigerator with a thoughtful expression, she said, "Andy might surprise you on this one."

"What makes you say that?"

"Because if he wants to be part of this child's life, he'll have to be accommodating."

"Maybe when he gets over his rush of paternal pride, he'll realize he doesn't want the responsibility. Maybe he'll bow out gracefully."

"Not likely considering the way he used to talk about having a child."

Meg sighed. "I don't think Andy really wanted a baby. He was just eager to find some way to put me under his thumb. A baby seemed the perfect solution. My job and my ambition challenged his masculine superiority. He wanted to put me in a nice, neat, traditional role. He was always that way. If I hadn't been so young and so blinded by lust, I would have seen our potential problems and never married him."

"Maybe Andy has changed."

"Get real," Meg said, rolling her eyes. "The man will never change. He's entirely predictable. The only thing that puzzles me is why he hasn't found some sweet little somebody to be at his beck and call twenty-four hours a day. If he really wanted a child he could have had one with someone else."

The look Perri sent her spoke volumes.

"You can stop looking at me that way. Andy is not still hung up on me. We've been through that before."

"But neither you nor he have been able to start a new life with anyone else."

Meg chose not to dwell on Perri's annoying, oft-repeated remark. "This isn't really about me or Andy. It's about this baby."

"A baby you would prefer to raise without a father."

Perri's soft words made Meg frown. Visions of a sad-eyed child asking questions about her absent father danced in her head. "That sounds different when I hear you say it."

"Does it make you think twice?"

"Maybe."

"It should," Perri said with spirit. She plucked an arm load of laundry from the basket that sat at her feet and with firm, precise movements, began sorting and folding baby clothes on the table. "For years women have been wanting fathers to become more involved in their children. But when Andy got excited about the child this afternoon, you became angry. A few months after the baby's born, when you've been up three nights in a row, you might be wishing you hadn't blocked him out. You might need some help."

A protest sprang readily to Meg's lips, but Perri cut her off. "Don't say you don't need anyone's help, Meg. You've never had a child."

"I have friends and a family. I'm sure my parents will help."

Perri raised one slim russet eyebrow. "Your mother is a full-time economics professor, your father is a tax attorney. When they're not working, they're off on some jaunt to the Caribbean. Do you really think they'll be around to help much when the baby has the colic?"

"A fat lot of good Andy would do me at a time like that, either," Meg insisted. "He'd probably be off playing cops and robbers. I don't need Andy."

"So you keep saying."

Pushing away from the table, Meg stood and went to the window behind the table. She opened the blinds wider and stared outside. "I really don't need a lecture about my failings with Andy."

But her friend wasn't through. "It seems to me that you spent entirely too much of your marriage trying to prove you didn't need him."

Stung by Perri's sharp tone, Meg turned around. "You never said that before."

Perri's smile was rueful. "Believe it or not, I do try to mind my business every once in a while."

"Really? I hadn't noticed." Sniffing, Meg folded her arms across her midriff and looked out the window again.

Setting aside the laundry, Perri joined her. "Oh, now, don't get mad. You know what I said is true."

"I can't undo the mistakes I made with Andy."

"I know." Perri slipped an arm around Meg's shoulders, and together they watched Perri's two little boys, who were roughhousing in the backyard sandbox. As she observed their antics, Perri's expression softened. "Your baby deserves two parents, Meg. Don't assume that your not needing Andy means the baby won't need him, too."

Meg pursed her lips. "I didn't really assume that. I went to see him today, didn't I? I told him what was going on."

"He'll want more than just knowing about it."

"I know."

The doorbell rang, and Perri groaned. "That's probably the kids from next door. They like to come over and destroy other people's houses. I'll get rid of them and be right back."

Meg leaned against the window casing. An unreasonable sense of loss filled her. Until today she had been able to pretend the baby was hers, all hers. And that pleased her. But it wasn't that simple. As Perri had said, Andy had a right to know his child. The baby had a right to a father. And that meant Andy was once again going to figure prominently in Meg's life.

"Once again?" she muttered. "He never stopped figuring prominently." Closing her eyes, she offered a silent prayer for the strength to get through this.

"It wasn't the next-door neighbors."

Turning at Perri's voice, Meg found Andy standing in the doorway that separated the kitchen and dining room. Her first reaction was anger, but she knew it was a wasted emotion at this point. So all she said was, "How'd you find me?"

Andy stepped into the room. "I'm a detective, remember?" His attempt at a smile was lopsided and faded fast. "We need to talk, Meg."

Perri bustled forward once more and swept her kitchen table clean. "Why don't the two of you have a seat? Andy, how about some lemonade or a beer?" From the nursery monitor on the counter, a baby's cry interrupted. Perri looked grateful for the excuse to leave as she unhooked the monitor and fled the room.

Taking hold of the back of a kitchen chair, Andy shook his head. "Old harum-scarum Perri has certainly settled down, hasn't she?" He bent to pick up a miniature football from the collection of toys littering the floor. "How many kids does she have?"

"Three." Meg didn't move from her spot near the window. Somehow standing made her feel more in control. "Perri's a great mother."

Nodding sagely, as if she had uttered some great truism, Andy said, "I think you'll be a great mother, too."

Meg wasn't quite able to meet his eyes. They were too blue, too intense. She hated the way her voice shook as she replied, "I'm going to do my best."

"Meg..."

She looked up. Andy had taken a seat, but he looked uncomfortable, sitting there in Perri's unfinished cane-backed chair, squeezing the toy ball in his hands. Feeling somewhat contrite about her earlier actions, Meg said, "I'm sorry I ran away from you."

"And I'm sorry about..." Andy looked even more ill at ease, and the ball he held went flat, its air escaping with a soft *whoosh.*

For some reason Meg found the leaking-air sound to be entirely appropriate. Part of the tension eased from her body as she smiled. "It's okay, Andy. No matter what I said back at the restaurant, I don't blame you for one of your...um..." She couldn't keep her smile from growing wider. "It isn't your fault one of your sperm escaped and swam upstream."

Andy dropped the ball, and his cheeks grew red. "That's not what I meant. I'm sorry because I didn't understand what you were telling me at first, about it being my..." his glance was apologetic "...that is, *our* baby."

"Maybe I wasn't being too clear." Meg stepped forward and leaned her arms on the back of the chair opposite his. "I've been so rattled lately that I don't always express myself too well."

"But you're feeling okay?"

She laughed at his almost comical concern. "Why is it that's the first thing people ask pregnant women?"

He grinned, too. "I don't know. It just seems appropriate."

"I feel great," Meg assured him. "So far, at least."

"Good. You look great. I mean, no one would think you were pregnant."

"It's kind of early for me to be showing. But I'll get as big as a house."

"I can't imagine that. But by—when is it due, anyway?"

"Mid-February, or so." Again she smiled. "I was able to pinpoint the conception date fairly accurately for the doctor."

Their laughter mingled, creating an atmosphere rife with intimacy. Andy sat forward, his features animated, eyes bright. "The whole time I was looking for you this afternoon, a million things were running through my mind about the baby. I know it's crazy considering he's not even born yet, but I keep thinking about Little League baseball and camp-outs and Boy Scouts...."

"What if he's a she?"

Andy shook his head. "Almost all the Baskins have boys. Dad had David and I, and I have a zillion male cousins and only two or three females—"

"This could be an exception. I have a feeling it's a girl."

"I won't argue the point now," Andy said good-naturedly, then sobered. "I know you said earlier that I shouldn't feel obligated, Meg, but—"

"That's right. I'm not assessing blame. That's not why I told you about the baby."

"Well, it isn't obligation I'm feeling." He stood, shoving his hands into his pockets. "I'm excited. I mean, I'm really, really excited."

"Tell me about it," she said sarcastically, thinking back to his antics on the street. "I thought you were going to become a traffic fatality."

"Yeah. My mind kept drifting while I was driving, too. I kept wanting to stop at phone booths and call everyone I know."

Instead of resenting his pride, this time Meg was pleased. Maybe Perri was right. Maybe this child was one thing she and Andy could agree upon. "I understand what you're feeling," she said, pulling the chair out from under the table. "After I accepted what was happening, I got so excited I went out and bought the baby a toy—a big, floppy-eared rabbit. It's so big the baby probably won't be able to play with it until she's five or six years old."

"I've been picking out names," Andy confessed, his grin reaching new dimensions of satisfaction. "Andrew Baskin, Junior. Or Hank Baskin, named for Hank Aaron, of course. Or maybe Max Baskin. I think that has a nice, ordinary Joe kind of..." His voice faded when he noticed Meg's smile had disappeared. "What's wrong?"

"The baby won't be named anything Baskin."

"What do you mean?"

"My name is Hathaway. The baby will have my name."

"But I'm the father."

"And we're not married."

"Not now, of course—"

"I never took your name."

"This time you should."

She stared at him openmouthed. "What?"

"This time you should take my name," Andy repeated. "It'll make it easier on the baby."

"Wait a minute," Meg said, waving her hand for him to stop. "What do you mean *this time?*"

"When we get married."

Face draining of color, Meg sat down in the chair. Hard.

Andy was beside her in a flash. "Meg, what's wrong? Are you okay? You look sick."

Rather forcefully, she pushed his hands away. A flush replaced her pallor. "Who said anything about marriage?"

"I assumed—"

"Wrong. You assumed wrong."

Straightening, Andy drew in a deep breath. "We have to get married, Meg."

"Who says?"

"We're having a baby. The right thing to do is to get married."

She hurtled out of the chair and paced across the kitchen, one fist pounding into her other hand for emphasis. "Oh, sure, two people who don't love each other and couldn't get along the first time should get remarried for the baby's sake. Some big favor we'd do the kid, Andy."

Anger sent the blood pumping through Andy's veins, but he struggled to hold on to his control. "If we don't get married, what will everyone say?"

"I wish you'd join the twentieth century. It is no longer the end of the world to have a child out of wedlock."

"Maybe not for movie stars and women whose clock is running out of time, but it's not for me." Andy jabbed a finger into his chest. "I don't want my kid growing up being called a bastard."

"Nobody will call her a bastard." Meg's dark eyes flashed fire. "Unless of course she takes after her father!"

Andy stared at her. "That wasn't necessary."

"Of course it wasn't," Meg admitted. Looking honestly sorry, she bit her lower lip. "I do lots of unnecessary things when I'm around you. I always have. That's why we shouldn't even try to raise this child together."

Her words snapped the grip he held on his control. Hands clenched at his sides, he stepped forward. "You're not going to keep me from my child, Meg."

She didn't back down in the face of his fury. "I don't want to keep you from your child!" she said, voice strident. "If, of course, you really want to participate. But I know how selfish you are. Once upon a time you said you really *wanted* our marriage to work.

Then you were never home. You were always off trying to get yourself killed—"

"That's unfair."

"No, it's the truth." Her voice didn't waver, even though she took a step backward as he came forward. "Are you planning to behave in the same way once our baby is born?"

"Why? Are you planning to quit your job?"

Her defiantly raised chin lifted another inch. "Of course not. And that has nothing to do with this."

"But how are you planning to raise a child and maintain your *precious* career?"

She threw up her hands. "Oh, yes, here we go. I was waiting for you to throw my career in my face."

"You've certainly never shied away from throwing mine up to me."

"It's different—"

He cut her off. "Yes, things that are important to you are always *different*, aren't they, Meg?"

She closed her eyes and took a deep breath. "I don't know why I'm even trying," she said tightly. "This is going to be a disaster. I'm going to spend the next eighteen years struggling to de-program all the sexist, small-minded ideas you implant in our baby's mind."

"I'm not sexist," Andy denied. "And equality goes both ways, Meg. That's one thing I've learned since we broke up. Apparently, you haven't."

"I always understood equality."

"Then prove it." Feeling as if he had gone a couple of rounds in the ring, the fight began to seep out of Andy, but his gaze didn't leave Meg's. "I have equal rights where the welfare of this child is concerned, and I think it's in the child's best interests for us to get married.''

"That's preposterous."

"Oh, come on, Meg." He was tired of this argument, just as he'd grown tired of all the arguments years ago. Why did everything with this woman have to be such a struggle? "A child needs a home, a family..."

"She'll have a home. We'll be a family. A different kind of family, but that's okay. There are millions of kids with parents who live apart."

"Yeah, I've arrested a few hundred of them."

"Dammit, Andy, that's stupid logic. Living with parents who don't love each other is just as damaging. Maybe more so."

"But we do care about each other," Andy protested. "We've always cared. If you didn't care, why did you see me all those times in the past few years? Hell, if I didn't care, why did I keep seeing you?"

The muscles worked in Meg's throat as she stared at him. "Caring isn't love, Andy. Think of how we argue. What good would that do any child?"

"Don't you think we could put some of our differences aside for the sake of our child?"

She shook her head, but Andy pressed on, reaching out to take her hand in his. "It's not as if everything between us has been bad. Think of the good times." His voice deepened. "Think of the night we made this baby."

The memory of that night hung between them, as clear as the minute they had moved into each other's arms. Andy could feel the current that had passed between them. He could taste Meg's lips, feel her hands on his body, hear her sighs of pleasure. They had been so in harmony that night. Whatever else might be said about this child, Andy knew it had been conceived in a spell of magic, an interlude of tenderness and passion.

As those memories flowed between them, he was sure Meg was going to capitulate. Her muscles relaxed. Her eyes softened. Then her resistance set in again. Shaking his hand off, she tried to edge past him. "This is too insane to even be talking about."

He stepped in front of her, catching her shoulders. "Marry me, Meg."

She shook him off. "No!"

"Dammit, Meg, you have to!"

She wheeled around to face him. "You seem to have forgotten a few things, Andy Baskin. The first of which is that I don't *have* to do anything."

When she had talked to him this way in the past, Andy had always wanted to throttle her. After all, it wasn't as if he had ever asked for blind obedience. Just a little compromise, a little give and take. Apparently that was still too much for her to handle. He executed a mocking bow. "Oh, yes, I forgot your title, Miss Independence. Shall I kneel and kiss the hem of your cloak of self-sufficiency?"

"Don't be a jackass, Andy."

"Then don't you be stupid. This is one time when relying on me shouldn't be so hard to do."

"I don't need you!" The minute the protest left Meg's lips, she looked over Andy's shoulder and saw Perri standing in the doorway. Her friend shook her head. For some reason that irritated Meg all the more.

"I'm leaving," she pronounced. "I'm going someplace where everyone isn't trying to tell me what to do!"

For the second time that day, she left Andy standing alone.

Meg went home, expecting to be followed. She wasn't.

The hours passed and Andy didn't show up. Even though she kept picking up the phone to see if it was working and peering through the windows in search of his car, he didn't come. The disappointment that engulfed Meg was a surprise. And it made her angrier than ever.

"I don't need him," she told the floppy-eared rabbit that reposed on her bed. "The baby and I don't need him at all."

The rabbit looked unconvinced.

Chapter Four

"So you just *demanded* that she marry you?"

"Yeah, that's right, Lisa," Andy returned sarcastically. "I asked the mother of my unborn child to be my wife. I thought I was doing the honorable thing."

"Man, sometimes you are so out of it." Slender legs crossed at the ankles, Lisa perched on a desk opposite Andy's. Her trim tangerine-colored suit complemented her blond hair, and even the harsh neon lights of the deserted precinct detectives' office didn't detract from her beautiful face. She looked more like a model than a police officer, except for the gun Andy knew she carried in her purse. In a pinch, he couldn't think of another officer he'd rather have backing him up. He also couldn't think of a better friend. Lisa had come by tonight to talk about an arson case she was on, but that had been shunted to the side in favor of Andy's problems with Meg.

"You blew this one, Hotshot," Lisa continued. "I'm taking Meg's side on this marriage proposal."

Andy snorted in disgust. "Thanks for the support, friend. And by the way, I really appreciate your running off and leaving me with her this afternoon at the restaurant."

Lisa tossed her head. "Oh, yes, I should have stayed. I'm sure Meg would have felt comfortable telling you she's pregnant while I occupied the third chair at the table."

"Okay, so you were right to leave."

"Big of you to admit it. It was obvious that she wanted to talk to you."

"Yeah, some talk. It was more like a bomb dropping."

"Which you compounded by tracking her down and *demanding* she marry you." Lisa shook her head. "Andy, didn't you learn anything when you were married to the woman? She isn't the kind of person who responds to demands."

He agreed with a morose nod. "She was pretty hot when she left. Her friend Perri suggested I get ready to do some serious on-my-knees groveling."

"I'll lend you some knee-pads."

"Perri thought the marriage idea was dumb, also."

"It's just not necessary."

"But after today I'll probably have to take Meg to court to get to see my own child." A new surge of anger accompanied the thought. Andy raked a hand through his hair.

Lisa slid off the desk. "That's not going to happen," she soothed. "I know Meg well enough to know she wouldn't do that." She moved behind Andy, and with the ease of long friendship began to massage his shoulders. "Just because Meg doesn't want to marry you doesn't mean you won't play a big part in the baby's life."

Andy flinched as Lisa's hands tried to work some of the tension from his tightened muscles. "I don't want to be a part-time father," he muttered. "I want to be there for my kid."

Lisa's massaging motion stilled. "A good part-time father beats the hell out of a lousy one who's around all the time."

Andy knew she was thinking about her ex-husband. But Andy was thinking of his own father. Karl Baskin was a hard worker, a good provider, a man faithful to his wife and respected by co-workers and neighbors. Not loved, however. Such a warm emotion could never be applied to Karl. He was a man who held himself tightly in check. And nothing Andy had ever done, especially after his brother died, had roused more than polite interest from Karl. That wasn't the kind of man or father Andy wanted to be.

"I really want this baby," he told Lisa again.

She leaned against his desk, her gaze thoughtful. "You're serious, aren't you?"

"Why do you sound so surprised? We've been talking about it for an hour now."

Lisa shrugged. "It's sometimes hard to tell what's really going on in your head."

"Oh, come on, I'm an open book."

"Sure, when it comes to those things you want people to know. The rest is off-limits."

Andy looked away. There was an element of truth in Lisa's words, but his problems in sharing his feelings with other people weren't something on which he wanted to dwell. "Now you sound like Meg."

"I always did think she had you pegged."

The springs in Andy's dilapidated desk chair creaked as he rocked back and folded his arms. "One thing Meg does know is that I'm stubborn. She knows I won't give up without a fight."

Lisa groaned. "Are you talking about this marriage thing again?"

"It's the right thing to do."

"It's a crock," Lisa shot back.

"But would you have a child out of wedlock?"

Her raised eyebrow gaze said it all. "You're asking the wrong person, Andy. You know I wish I'd never married the jerk."

"You weren't pregnant when you married him, either."

"If I had been, I would never have married him for that reason alone."

Andy didn't believe her. "You say that now...."

"It's the truth. A baby is no reason to get married. It's not even a reason to stay married. Remember? I had Terry as a last-ditch attempt to save my marriage. And it only made things worse."

He accepted most of what Lisa was saying, but still insisted, "Meg and I have a responsibility to do right by this child."

Lisa straightened from the desk. "Yes, you have a responsibility. A child needs love, care, encouragement and opportunities. Nowhere is it written that two parents have to be married in order to provide those things."

"But marriage would make it easier for me to have a genuine role in my child's life."

"Easy isn't always an option, Andy." Lisa shoved her hands into her jacket pockets as she paced away from the desk. "On nights like tonight when I have to work, it would be easier if I had a husband who wanted to be part of my kid's life. It would be easier if my marriage had been fairy-tale perfect. It would be easier if you and Meg had never broken up before."

"Talk about fairy tales," Andy scoffed.

"Right," Lisa said. "But this isn't a fairy tale. And what you have to deal with is reality."

He sat still for a moment then exhaled slowly. His admission of failure came hard. "Meg isn't going to marry me."

"I think it's good that you realize that. Because, frankly..." Lisa's words trailed off, her gaze faltered and fell.

"Frankly what?"

She cleared her throat and continued, "I don't know if you'll ever be ready for marriage."

Silence reigned for a minute and stretched into two.

"I'm trying to be candid," Lisa said.

"Well." Andy shifted in his chair again. "It's nice to know how I'm regarded."

Lisa's hands went to her hips. "Let's face it, Hotshot. You're not exactly batting a thousand in the relationship department."

"So I'm divorced...."

"And you've left a trail of women behind you that would stretch from here to Peachtree Center."

"That's an exaggeration."

"Not by much. And why is it, do you think, that none of these women has managed to meet your rigorous qualifications for marriage?"

Andy sat up straighter. "Don't start with me about equality and women's rights. I've changed my tune—"

"Yes, yes," Lisa interrupted. "I know you're not the same traditional-minded chauvinist you used to be."

"You're damn straight," he said. "I mean, I acknowledge what women can do. Just look at you—you're a great cop, a terrific mother, you were even a good wife to that unappreciative jerk. In the past few years I've seen lots of women who do a great balancing act between families and careers. I'm not so hung up on that stuff anymore."

Lisa nodded her head. "I know you've changed, Andy. I'm willing to admit you've almost caught up with the rest of the world."

"If Meg would ever really listen to me, she'd realize that, too."

"Which brings us back to where we started this conversation," Lisa said smugly. "I'm sure your ranting and raving and demanding that she marry you really convinced Meg that you're a changed man."

Andy flushed. "I guess you're right again."

"But your attitude about a woman's place in the world isn't what's kept you from relationships. It's what we were talking about before—it's the way you hold yourself back."

Andy turned away from Lisa. "Could we stop dissecting my personality for a while?"

"What did the last woman who broke up with you say?"

Busily and blindly sifting through a stack of reports on his desk, Andy ignored her.

Lisa went around the desk and, with hands braced on the front edge, leaned forward till her face was close to his. "She said you were remote, didn't she? She said though you had a lot of laughs together, she never really felt as if she knew you. Isn't that right?"

Unable to avoid his friend's probing gaze, Andy looked up. "Someday I'll learn not to go for beers with you when I'm nursing a broken heart."

Laughter bubbled from Lisa as she straightened. "Your heart hasn't been broken since Meg walked out. Your heart hasn't been deeply involved enough to break."

Spinning away from Lisa, Andy flipped the switch on the computer terminal next to his desk. "I have work to do," he muttered. "Don't you?"

At the other end of the room, a door banged open and admitted Will Espinoza, Andy's new partner of only six weeks.

Tall and dark, with handsome features that bespoke his Cuban heritage, Will stalked toward Andy and Lisa, scowling. "Sounds like you're having a party," he said. "How come I wasn't invited?"

"Because we wanted to have fun," Lisa retorted. She and Will always seemed to rub each other the wrong way.

Andy spoke up before anything could ignite between them. "You seem to be in a delightful mood, partner."

"Probably because I spent all afternoon—*alone*—chasing down leads in the Hollingsworth case."

Guiltily Andy recalled the full afternoon of work he and Will had planned. "I'm sorry. Something came up."

After tossing his rumpled jacket onto a chair, Will waited expectantly. "Well?"

"It was personal."

"And that's an excuse?"

Andy glanced at Lisa, then back to Will. "It was important, okay? What have you got on—"

"I've got nothing," Will shot back, snatching up his coat again. "For you I've got nothing."

"Oh, come on, Will, man, I'm sorry."

Will glared at him. "Good. Then you can explain to the Captain why our caseload is piling up to the ceiling. I don't know what's with you, man, but whatever it is, I hope you get it figured out real soon."

"We'll work it out. I said I was sorry."

But Will dismissed Andy and started for the door, pausing only once to say, "And to think I was looking forward to working with one of the department's living legends. Ha!"

Lisa, always quick to defend a friend, started forward. "Hey, Espinoza, you'd better watch—" The slam of the door cut off her warning.

She wheeled back to face Andy. "Who does he think he is?"

"Some guy whose partner let him down, I'd guess."

"He's just a punk."

"He's a damn good detective. And I owe him some kind of explanation for today." Sighing, Andy sank down in his chair. He owed Will an explanation for more than today. Ever since that night with Meg, he hadn't been giving his work the hundred percent it deserved. In all the years he'd been a cop, he had prided himself on not letting personal problems get in the way of his job. But lately he had spent a lot of time questioning the life choices he had made. When he should have been working on a case, he had found himself gazing off into space, thinking about calling Meg, feeling lonely and dissatisfied. Today, in the face of Meg's news, he had forgotten everything else. It bothered him. He wasn't accustomed to letting his partners down.

Lisa came up beside him and touched his shoulder. "Andy—"

"Let's not to talk about it anymore, okay?" he said. "I'll deal with Meg and the baby tomorrow. Wasn't there a case you wanted to discuss?"

Though Lisa seemed reluctant to let things drop, she didn't push. Instead she said, "Captain Hughes said for me to run this by you..." She went on to give Andy the background details on a recent fire.

Andy listened, taking in all the pertinent details of a fire at an unfinished office complex. It was obviously arson, but there appeared to be no motive from the development company which would benefit in the insurance settlement. The head of the firm was in excellent financial shape, and his sister and his son, who were his partners, had died in the blaze. No one seemed to know why the two were at the complex. All the facts seemed to indicate they were the arsonists, caught by mistake in their own scheme, but there still remained the matter of motive. Lisa's instincts said there was some other element, and what looked like an accidental death could have been murder....

"...don't you think?"

Blinking, Andy looked up at Lisa. Somewhere toward the end of her story, his mind had shifted to Meg. "I'm sorry, I didn't..."

In answer, Lisa said, "Go home, Andy. Get some rest. Go over to Meg's and get something resolved in the morning. We'll talk about this case when your mind is clearer."

It was good advice. The day's events had left him wound as tight as a clock. But at home in his comfortable old recliner, with Boomer resting by his side on the floor, Andy couldn't relax. He kept thinking about what Lisa had said about his inability to open up to anyone. He'd heard the same from Meg and from more than one woman he had dated. Years ago, after he was involved in a shoot-out where he killed a man, Andy had, as decreed by departmental regulations, seen a psychologist. After several less-than-productive meetings, the doctor told him he seemed to have a fear of displaying too much emotion, an inability to let anyone get too close.

At the time, Andy had told the doctor he was full of beans. But lately the psychologist's words had returned to bother him. The man people kept describing him as sounded more like his father than himself.

Oh, he wasn't obviously like his father. He wasn't somber and taciturn. He got some joy out of living. But he could now admit to himself that he had a problem with intimacy. Even to Lisa, who was without equal the closest friend he'd ever had, he didn't reveal all he was feeling. Until tonight, he hadn't known she was on to him about that.

When it came to romantic relationships, the problem was worse. It wasn't a problem with sex. In fact, Andy had learned how to use sex as a shield. When the physical relationship was good, it could disguise other problems, create a false sense of intimacy. The illusion eventually shattered, of course. Sex hadn't been enough to cement any of the relationships he had attempted. It hadn't been enough for Meg, even though she was the one woman he had really loved. Lisa had hit the bull's-eye on that one tonight, too. Meg was the only woman who had ever gotten close enough to break his heart.

Groaning, Andy laid his head back against the decade-softened leather of his chair. Boomer, loyal dog that he was, got up and pushed his nose against Andy's hand.

"Yeah, Boom, old boy," Andy said as he stroked the setter's head, "I'm your basic screwed-up mess. No wonder Meg doesn't want to marry me again."

Now, in the calm aftermath of Meg's shocking news, Andy could admit his remarriage idea was wrong. Yes, he'd like his child to carry his name. Absolutely, he wanted to be a real parent. But marriage? What had made him think it would work? Why had he gone off on such a tangent about it?

There was only one possible answer.

Which he told Meg the next morning.

"You make me nuts," he said the minute she answered her doorbell. "You always have."

Staring at Andy, Meg held on to the doorknob as if it were a lifeline. She clutched at the neck of her silky yellow robe with her other hand and shook her head in an attempt to clear the haze from in front of her eyes. "What . . . what time is it, anyway?"

Andy frowned at her. "It's nearly seven-thirty. I thought you'd be ready for work. Or don't you still get to your desk by eight-fifteen?"

"I . . ." Meg swallowed, trying to conquer the black hole of nausea that threatened to engulf her. "I'm running a little late," she finally whispered.

"Do I have to wait out here?" Andy asked.

"No...no, I'm sorry." She fell back to allow him entry into her condo's foyer. The click of the door seemed to echo like a gunshot in her head.

"Anyway," Andy continued as he preceded her into the living room. "What I'm saying is that I was wrong yesterday. We probably shouldn't get married. But you always make me crazy, Meg, you know that. I don't behave in a rational manner when you..." Turning, he peered at her in concern. "Are you all right?"

Nodding took all her strength. She grabbed the back of a wing chair to shore herself up. "It's good...good to hear you've come to your sense...senses."

"Meg?"

I will not be sick, she vowed to herself, *I will not be so weak in front of him.* But in the next second she was bolting for the powder room off the foyer. There she was so violently and completely ill that she didn't realize Andy had followed her until he pressed a cool, damp washcloth to her forehead.

Sprawled on the floor with the flushing of the toilet providing background music, she tried to retain some semblance of dignity. "I'm sorry, I don't know..." When Andy chuckled, she glared at him.

"Oh, now," he soothed. "It's not as if I haven't seen you with your head in the toilet before."

"That's not true."

"Remember New Year's Eve nine years ago?"

Groaning, she held the washcloth to her burning face. "Oh, God, I had forgotten that."

He closed the toilet seat and sat down, his brows drawing together as he studied her. "Yesterday you said you were feeling okay."

"I was." She leaned her head against the wall and frowned at him again. It was just her luck to have her first bout of morning sickness on the day Andy appeared on her doorstep.

"You don't look okay."

"Thanks for the compliment."

"You want some crackers or something?"

Her stomach rolled at the suggestion, and she waved him out of the way as another tide of nausea swept through her. Afterward, when she leaned against the wall, she said, "Could you leave or something? I'd rather be sick in private."

Andy looked insulted. "I can't leave you like this."

"Why not?"

"You might need me."

Her classic comeback was lost in another surge of sickness. But at least Andy left the powder room. She heard the phone ringing and Andy answering it, but she was too weak to care. Later, he appeared with another washcloth and a soft drink, both of which she accepted gratefully. And she had to admit to appreciating the strength he provided as he guided her to the couch in the sun room off the kitchen. Briefly she thought about the night before, when she'd been so sure she didn't need Andy. Today it felt good to have him around.

He arranged the couch's colorful throw pillows to cushion her head, slanted the blinds to redirect the morning sun and provided still another damp cloth for her forehead. He even sat down on the floor next to the couch. "Are you feeling any better?"

She nodded then frowned at his concerned expression. "What are you doing?"

"Taking care of you."

"I know. But why?"

"Isn't that obvious? You're sick."

"But you hate sick people."

He shrugged and changed the subject. "Your office called. I told them you weren't feeling well."

"Oh, God." Meg squeezed her eyes shut. "The Jenkins account. I had a big meeting scheduled for this morning. What time is it?"

"Your secretary said she'd cancel everything until afternoon."

"No," Meg said, struggling to get up. "I'm fine now, and—"

"Everything's already canceled. Why don't you relax?"

Giving up, she sank back against the bright floral upholstery. "What'd my secretary say?"

"Well, at first she didn't believe I was your ex-husband."

"She's new," Meg said. "I probably haven't mentioned you to her."

"Have you mentioned the baby to anyone?"

She shook her head. "I only told you yesterday, remember?"

He exhaled. "Yeah, I remember. There are lots of things about yesterday that I'd like to forget, however."

Meg waited for him to elaborate, but he didn't even meet her gaze. He got up, took off his navy sport coat and gun holster and went into the kitchen. She heard ice clinking into a glass from the dispenser on the refrigerator door. Water gurgled. Then Andy reappeared in the kitchen doorway. "You want some water?"

She shook her head. He drained the glass and returned it to the kitchen. Then he was back again, looking even more nervous than before.

Meg watched him pace around the room. His masculine presence, including the gun and holster he had laid on a nearby chair, was at odds with the wicker-filled, green- and yellow-hued room. Funny, she hadn't noticed how feminine this space was until seeing Andy here. Like a caged panther, he continued to pace until she asked, "Shouldn't you be at work?"

"I called my partner and told him not to expect me for a while."

"Why?"

"You might need—"

"I'm okay, Andy," Meg said, pushing herself to a sitting position again. "And that doesn't really answer my question. Why are you here?"

"I told you."

She laughed shortly. "You once went to work and left me home in bed with a hundred-and-five-degree temperature."

He loosened his red-striped tie, looking uncomfortable. "Maybe my priorities are a little more in order than they used to be."

She was silent.

"Don't you see?" Andy said. "I've changed a lot."

"Then why is it we always end up in an argument about the same things we always argued about?"

"It's what I said earlier. You make me crazy."

She started to say that was no excuse, but then reconsidered. For Andy made her crazy, too. He seemed able to push all her buttons, to make her angrier—and happier, she had to admit—than any person she had ever known. He had always forced her to respond in uncharacteristically irrational ways. It was those extremes in herself and in him that she had been most unable to live with.

But that wasn't important now. Last night, as she had waited for him to follow her, Meg had done some hard thinking. Everything Perri had said to her yesterday was true; this baby deserved a father. Meg needed to stop behaving childishly and reach some compromise with Andy.

Toward that end, she took a deep, calming breath and said, "All right, Andy, if you say you've changed, I believe you."

"And I can be a good father to our child."

She took another breath then nodded. "Okay, I believe that, too."

"But yesterday you—"

"Yesterday I was just about as out of control as you were."

He took a seat in the fan-backed wicker chair facing the couch. "I'm really sorry for the way I behaved yesterday. Have you talked to Perri?"

"She thinks we're both idiots."

He nodded. "She might be right. I ran out of there like a cat with its tail on fire."

Meg smiled. "Perri was afraid you were going to track me down and drag me by the hair of my head to a justice of the peace."

"Real caveman stuff, huh?"

"She told me I deserved whatever you did to me."

Andy looked surprised.

"Perri agrees with you," Meg said. "She thinks I've been waving the independence banner too long and too hard."

"That surprises me. Back when we were married, the two of you used to gang up on me about feminism and equality."

Meg swung her feet to the floor as she replied, "Perri doesn't think we should get married just because of the baby. But she has three kids. She says it would be better for me and the baby if I start sharing this with you."

"She's right." Andy left his chair and joined Meg on the couch. His expression was very solemn. "The getting-married stuff was a knee-jerk reaction, Meg. Marrying you again would be the worst mistake I could make."

"Gee," Meg said dryly. "Thanks...I think."

"You know what I mean," Andy returned. "We screwed it up pretty bad before."

"And we would again." Meg didn't know why those words—the unvarnished, complete truth—caused her chest to tighten. Nor did she understand why she had such a hard time gazing into Andy's blue eyes for any length of time. In the face of pregnancy and morning sickness and for the sake of their child, one would think she could summon up the least bit of indifference to his man. But the only thing she knew for certain was she didn't like sitting so close to him. So she got up. Quickly. And for a moment the room swam before her eyes.

"Hey," Andy said softly, standing up to steady her. "You need to sit down and take it easy."

Meg's head cleared. "I'm fine," she insisted, and took a tentative step away from him. "See, I'm all right."

His gaze was skeptical. "Maybe you shouldn't go into the office at all today."

"It's just morning sickness. It'll pass."

He shoved his hands into the pockets of his khaki slacks, exactly as he always did when he was nervous. Meg drew her robe tighter around her body. She cleared her throat. "Well, I'm glad we're in agreement about the marriage."

"There are some other things we ought to work out."

"Like what?"

"Money, for one thing."

"Money?"

"For doctor's bills, clothes, baby furniture, things you'll need."

"Andy, I'm more than capable—"

"I know you're capable," he cut in. Meg stiffened at his tone. He began again, "It doesn't have anything to do with your capabilities. I'm sure you make a lot more money than I do, and once upon a time that would have bothered me."

"It doesn't now?"

"Not really. I figure, what does it matter, anyway?"

Surprised, she studied his face for signs of insincerity. They weren't apparent. "You mean that, don't you?"

"Yes, I do. But that doesn't mean I don't want to share the expense of our child with you. And take note, Meg," he said, his cocky grin appearing. "I said *share*. Equality, remember?"

She found herself smiling back. "Yeah, I remember."

"Then that's settled."

She nodded.

"And there are some legalities I want to clear up."

"Legalities?"

Andy shifted from foot to foot and cleared his throat. "This isn't something that's easy to discuss, Meg, but...well...what if something happened to you?"

"What do you mean?"

"After the baby's born," he continued, his voice husky. "If anything happened to you, I wouldn't want there to be any question about who the baby would go to."

She had a sudden, startling vision of herself lying injured or dead and her baby, crying somewhere, all alone. Instinctively she pressed a hand to her stomach.

"He'd belong with me," Andy whispered. "I want to make sure that's clear, Meg. I mean, I know I was never your family's favorite person. Especially after we broke up."

"That's not really true—"

He brushed her protest aside. "That's not important. What matters is that I wouldn't want them or anyone else to question my rights where this child will be concerned. I'd fight for him, Meg."

Startled by the depth of emotion in his voice, she stared at Andy. Weeks ago, when the baby had become a reality to her, she had understood, as she hadn't before, why someone would lay down their life for their child. The feeling was unlike any other love Meg had ever known. She loved her parents, her brother and sister. She thought of Perri as more a sister than merely a friend. She had adored her grandmother Kathy. And once, years ago, she had loved Andy. But this feeling, this fervor, was an altogether different emotion. An emotion that, apparently, Andy shared.

"It's funny, isn't it?" she asked quietly, her hand still pressed to her stomach. "It's funny how strongly you can feel about a tiny little scrap of humanity."

Andy nodded. His eyes were very blue, very bright. "Only yesterday I wouldn't have thought it possible to feel so much for a child that's not even born."

"The feeling overwhelms you, doesn't it?"

"And that's why..." Andy swallowed before he continued. "That's why I want it clear, Meg. I never want anything to happen to you—"

"I know that—"

"But if it did, I'd be there for the child. I'll be there regardless—"

"Of course you will." Meg wasn't sure if she believed those words before she said them. But she did now. She knew Andy was sincere. He'd be there for their child. And she was profoundly ashamed when she remembered considering not telling him about the baby. She realized now how selfish that would have been.

Smiling though her lips trembled, she took his hand. "I'll make sure, Andy. You'll be listed on the birth certificate as the father, of course, but I'll go to a lawyer, make a will, do something. We'll do this right. We'll even..." She took a deep breath, then plunged ahead with the decision she had reached before Andy had even shown up this morning. "We'll hyphenate the baby's last name, if that's all right with you."

"Hyphenate?"

"Baskin, dash, Hathaway. Does that sound okay?"

"Well." Dropping her hand, he rubbed his chin. "It's different."

"I think it's downright regal."

"He'll probably get into a couple of fights at school when the kids tease him and tell him he has a weird name."

"You would think of that."

"But I can probably teach him to defend himself."

"Or I'll teach *her* to ignore small-minded punks."

Andy grinned. "Between the two of us, he or she should be prepared for anything."

"All we can do is try."

"I want to do that." His grin disappeared. "I want to try and do this right. I know you said yesterday that I'm always off trying to get myself killed."

"I told you I didn't mean all the things I said yesterday."

"But you've always thought I took too many chances. And there was a time when you were right." Andy took her hand again. "But not now, Meg. Lisa may still call me 'Hotshot,' but that's not the way I operate. And now..." His gaze dropped from her eyes to her stomach. "Now I have more reason than ever to stay alive."

The memory of Andy taking off after the purse snatcher was still too vivid for Meg to believe everything he said. The faint pink scar under his jaw gave testimony to his propensity to land in trouble. But she didn't want to argue the point now. She hoped those arguments were in the past. From now on, she wanted to concentrate on getting along with her child's father. Smiling, she began, "Well, *Dad*... "

The word brought Andy's grin back. "Yes, *Mom?*"

They laughed together, and once again, Meg became all too aware of Andy's proximity. His hand was big and warm, enclosing hers. She could smell his after-shave, the same citrusy blend he had used when they were married. She found it pleasant, as she always had. But she resisted the pull the scent exerted on her senses. She tugged her fingers free, stepped back and again tightened the sash on her robe.

Andy's gaze had gone back to her stomach. "You know, you still don't look pregnant."

She felt suddenly self-conscious. Her laughter sounded a little too bright. "Not much has changed since you said that yesterday, Andy. And I am only ten weeks along, but there is this tiny little bulge."

"Really?" Andy's eyes widened.

His regard made her turn away. "It's not much of a bulge, really—" She jumped as Andy's arms slid around her waist. "Andy, what are you—"

"What bulge?" he asked as his fingers splayed across her lower belly. She felt the warmth of his hand through the thin silk of her robe. "I don't feel a bulge."

"Andy!" She twisted out of his arms. "What do you mean grabbing me like that?"

"I want to feel my baby."

"The baby can't be felt yet."

"But you said there was a bulge."

"It's tiny. I'm probably the only one who would notice. It's not something you can feel through my clothes."

Andy's next suggestion was apparent by the look in his eyes.

Meg cheeks grew warm. "Andy!"

"Well, it's not as if I haven't seen you without your clothes before."

"You won't again."

"But I want to see the baby growing."

"I don't think it's something I can hide."

"I don't want to see just what everyone else can." His tone deepened as he wheedled, "Come on, Meg . . ."

"Forget it. Taking my clothes off was what got me in this situation." She brushed a hand through her hair. "We're going to get along for the sake of the baby. But I'm not going to get into that kind of thing with you, Andy. Sex has always complicated things for us. This time we're going to live up to that vow we made about being grown-ups."

"But this isn't sex," Andy said. "This is sharing. I want to share it all with you. Every change in your body. Every stage of the pregnancy."

"I'll tell you every time my stomach grows a quarter of an inch."

"It's not the same." He took a deep breath. "Don't you understand, Meg? This is probably the only baby I'll ever have."

"You're only thirty-four years old. Your opportunities are limitless."

"But what if they're not?" he demanded. "What if I miss all this now and never get it back?"

As always, Andy could paint a convincing picture. Meg did her best to resist his pleading glance. "I doubt if a bulging stomach will be as exciting as you're imagining."

"Let me be the judge." Before she knew his intention his hand went back to her stomach.

And this time Meg didn't move away. She stood still, her eyes on Andy's face as his fingers pressed against her. There was such wonder in his expression. Such tenderness. She couldn't help her reaction. She was moved beyond all comprehension, so moved that tears filled her eyes.

"Andy," she whispered.

He looked up, his wonder quickly changing to concern. "Meg?"

"We're having a baby, Andy."

His smile reappeared. "Yeah," he murmured. "Yeah, we are."

Meg hugged him then. In a patch of sunshine that slanted through the blinds, she hugged him hard.

But as he held Meg tight, it wasn't the baby Andy was thinking of. It was how right she had always felt in his arms. And the way he touched her, which hadn't been about sex at all, changed. Even though he wanted to behave like a grown-up, he found himself wishing they could go upstairs, where he could bury himself in Meg's sweet, welcoming depths. That impulse, however, was one he knew he wouldn't follow.

Not today, anyway.

Chapter Five

The midmorning sunshine turned Perri's hair into a flaming halo around her face as she crossed the deck and dropped into the lounge chair next to Meg's. "I can't get over how great Andy is with Jocelyn."

Meg nodded, pretending to flip through the book in her lap as she followed Andy's progress around her small backyard. He carried Perri's daughter, now a plump four-and-a-half-month-old, and was explaining to the gurgling baby the various plants and shrubs they were encountering. For a Saturday in mid-August the temperature was moderate, the air was filled with the fresh scents of flowers and new-mown grass. Both man and child seemed to be enjoying their stroll.

"Jocelyn loves grass," Andy called up to Perri.

"Just don't let her eat any."

"I won't. We're going around to the front, though."

"Look at him," Meg muttered as he disappeared from view. "He's a regular baby expert."

Perri slipped her sunglasses down her nose to peer at Meg over the lenses. "Trouble in Baby Wonderland?"

Meg wrinkled her nose. "Sounds like the title of a trite television movie, doesn't it?"

"Your life is a television movie," Perri countered, settling back in her chair with a sigh. "Man, this is great. The boys are with Rod. I can just lie back here in the sun. You'll find out how precious leisure time is once the baby's here, Meg."

"I'm sure Mr. Baby Expert will always be available to take my child off my hands."

Perri tsk-tsked. "Meg, instead of complaining, you should be happy that everything's working out so well with Andy."

"I know, I know. He's being really supportive. He calls me several times every day to see how I'm feeling. At least three nights a week, he comes over to discuss baby names or just to talk to my stomach."

Perri giggled. "What does he say?"

"Well, last night he recited the career batting averages of all his favorite baseball players."

"That's not so bad. Rod read *War and Peace* to all three of ours."

Meg rolled her eyes. "Andy is out of control. He has barred all forms of caffeine—other than chocolate, which I told him I *had* to have—from my house and office. He read somewhere that it wasn't good for pregnant women or babies. He was probably on a search-and-destroy mission when he got here today. He had that kind of intense look in his eyes."

"I think he's being very sweet."

"Yeah, sweet." Meg closed her book with a little bang. "His baby is the most important thing in the world."

After a slight hesitation, Perri murmured, "Sounds as if Mommy Meg is jealous."

"That's absurd." As usual, her observant friend had struck a little too close to the truth for comfort. The irrational, irrelevant feelings of jealousy Meg had been experiencing weren't something she wanted to discuss. "I told you he went to the doctor with me this week, didn't I?"

"You didn't go into any details."

"We heard the heartbeat for the first time. You'd have thought this was the first time a baby's heartbeat had ever been heard. He did one of those little dances, you know, like football players do when they score a touchdown."

Perri laughed. "I wish I'd seen that."

Meg glared at her. "It was embarrassing. I'll bet people heard him carrying on all the way out in the waiting room."

"Oh, Meg, give him a break. Weren't you excited, too?"

"Yes—"

"Then surely you can't fault Andy for being a little foolish. That's a pretty big moment."

Opening her book again, Meg said, "Maybe I'm kind of tired of him being at my side every time I turn around. Look at the way he turned up here this morning without even calling. And just when I was set for a nice visit with you and Jocelyn. I wish he'd give me a minute—just one minute—to myself."

"Do you?"

The disbelieving note in her friend's voice made Meg look up. She had never been able to fool Perri, especially about Andy. "What does that mean?"

Green eyes dancing with laughter, Perri anchored her sunglasses in her hair. "I've been wondering when *it* was going to surface."

"What's *it?*"

"Sex, of course. In the past eight years, you and Andy have rarely seen each other without jumping into the nearest bed. Afterward, you'd both scurry off to your respective corners, gathering strength for the next round. Being with him all the time must create a lot of tension."

Meg studied the hem of her white cotton jumper and avoided Perri's gaze. "Sex is no longer a problem."

"Oh, really? And how did you manage to conquer the beast of lust?"

"We've simply agreed not to let it be an issue."

Perri hooted with laughter. "That's bull, Meg."

"What?"

"Hey, this is me, Perri, your best friend. I know things about you and Andy. Remember, I've been with you when keeping your eyes and your hands off each other was pretty darned tough.''

"It isn't tough now," Meg said firmly. "Andy is behaving himself and I'm...I'm not interested in sex. I feel like this big, unattractive cow." That wasn't the truth in the strictest sense of the word, but it was all Perri needed to know.

Sitting up, Perri gave her a critical once-over. "I hate to break this to you, Meg, but you're not even showing yet."

"That's not what my mother said."

"Your mother?" Perri gave her a blank look, then clapped a hand to her forehead. "Oh, my God, Meg, when Andy showed up and started playing with Jocelyn, I completely forgot to ask you about last night. Did Andy go with you to tell your parents?"

"You make it sound as if we're a couple of teenagers in trouble."

"Isn't that how you felt?"

"Of course," Meg admitted with a faint smile. She had felt very young last night when she faced her mother and father. And instead of wishing he would disappear, she had been happy to have Andy with her. In fact, it had been at Andy's prodding that she had finally stopped putting off the unavoidable and gone to talk with her parents about the baby. She had been dreading the moment. Andy had understood that—he still hadn't told his parents, either. And last night, his presence had made the ordeal much easier to get through. It was that reliance on him, a habitual situation these days, that had helped put Meg in a bad mood this morning.

"What did your parents say?" Perri prompted.

"They were surprised to see Andy."

"You didn't warn them?"

Meg shook her head. "Surprise attacks are always the best when dealing with my parents. I waited until I knew they'd be through with dinner, but before they usually bury themselves in reading or paperwork."

"What'd they say?"

"They were shocked. Dad looked a little like he did the night I told him I wasn't going to law school."

"Your mother?"

"She assumed the whole thing had been planned, of course. Mother plans everything. She assumes her children do, too."

Perri shrugged. "You always did plan things." She grinned. "Until you met Andy."

Meg leaned her head back against the chair and exhaled slowly. Yes, Andy had been—and still was—the one aberration in the life her parents had envisioned for her, the life she had planned for herself. Like her brother and sister, she had been encouraged, expected to do well in school, to have a successful career. In addition to those accomplishments, her siblings also had good marriages and families. Instead, Meg was now embarking on unmarried motherhood with her ex-husband. She didn't really blame her father for looking momentarily disappointed. And she had to give him credit for recovering his poise in a hurry.

"Did your dad treat Andy okay?" Perri asked.

"Everyone thought Dad didn't like Andy when we were married," Meg retorted. "And it wasn't that at all. What he didn't like was how quickly we married."

"So he was nice last night?"

"He was wonderful. And Mother . . . Mother acted thrilled about the baby."

"I don't know why I expected anything else. Your mother is the original liberated woman. Remember when she burned our training bras when we were in the sixth grade?"

"And your parents didn't allow you to come over for months."

Perri laughed in delight. "I love your mom."

"She's pretty neat," Meg agreed. "She acted great about this whole thing. But I didn't enlighten her about the pregnancy being an accident. I think she found it much easier to think that I reached a certain age, wanted a child and decided to have it with Andy, a man I already know. That appeals to her independent nature and her logical mind."

"Nobody mentioned marriage?"

"Not even Andy."

"You're lucky," Perri proclaimed. "I'm thirty-two, but if I were having a baby without being married, my parents would be breaking out the shotguns for a wedding."

"Dad and Andy had brandy and cigars."

"And a damn fine cigar it was," Andy said, appearing on the deck steps. He was holding the baby away from his chest. "Perri, your daughter is leaking."

Intentionally avoiding his gaze, Meg picked up her book again. "You mean you can't change her, Andy?" she demanded in mock horror. "I'm surprised."

He didn't catch her sarcasm. "I guess I could. Show me how, Perri?"

Meg waited until they had disappeared inside the condo to throw her book aside once more. *Babies,* she fumed silently. As excited as she was about the child she was carrying, she yearned for one moment when the entire conversation didn't center around babies. It was as if she didn't exist anymore.

"Hey, Mom!"

Andy's teasing tone as he called to her from the sun room only added to her impatience. "I'm not your mother," Meg snapped, getting to her feet. She stalked down the deck stairs and into the yard.

"What'd I say?" Andy said, turning to Perri.

"I think our Meg is overdosing on baby talk."

He nodded, pretending to understand, even though he didn't. He thought Meg wanted to talk about babies. Silently he followed Perri's diapering instructions, all the while wondering about Meg's outburst. When Jocelyn began to protest his amateurish efforts, Perri nudged him to the side.

"Don't worry," she told Andy. "Meg will be fine. But you might want to lighten up about the baby stuff for a while."

And do what? Andy wondered. If he wasn't talking about the baby or making plans for the baby, he wouldn't have any real reason to be around Meg. No reason he could reveal to her, anyway. And he wanted to be with her. As hard as he fought their old, irrational attraction, it still kept popping up.

He wanted to hear her laughter, see her tip-tilted nose as it wrinkled when she was displeased. He wanted to smell the floral fragrance of her perfume. But those desires weren't ones he was supposed to have. Despite the incendiary nature of their past relationship, they were supposed to deal with each other coolly. He and Meg were grown-ups. She had made it clear that there'd be no giving in to passion again. The baby was their only connection now. And in the past few weeks, the baby had drawn them closer than they had ever been. So Andy had been making the most of that connection. He thought he wanted to build on it.

But what now?

Unsure of what he should say, he was quiet when Meg came inside. Whatever had been bothering her before seemed to have passed, because her smile was once more in place. She seemed calm and in control and so very, very beautiful. Last night Meg's mother had said pregnancy was bringing a bloom to her cheeks. Andy had to agree. In her simple loose-fitting white dress with her hair pulled back from her face, she shone with healthy, radiant beauty. His heart filled to bursting when he watched her with Jocelyn in her arms, but he didn't say anything. The words "baby" or "pregnancy" never once passed his lips. He was afraid he would say something that would put her in an ill humor again. So when Perri and her daughter were gone, he started to leave also.

Meg looked surprised. "Wasn't there something you wanted to talk to me about, Andy?"

He studied the tips of his worn leather running shoes for a moment. "It's nothing..."

"But when you got here you looked really serious."

"It's not important."

"Andy," she said with a long-suffering expression. "I know when you want to talk. Now what is it?"

Shoving his hands into the pockets of his faded blue shorts, he said, "I figured that since your parents know about the baby—" he darted a quick look at her face for signs of irritation "—then perhaps I should tell mine."

Meg nodded.

"So I'm going over there this afternoon. And I just thought..." He paused, changing his mind about the whole thing. "I thought I'd stop over here first," he finished lamely. "To see how you're doing."

Her eyes narrowed. "That's the only reason you came by?"

"Yeah, I mean...no." Andy took a deep breath and plunged ahead, "What I mean is that I'd like you to go with me."

Meg could see how hard it was for Andy to ask. He might have altered some of his opinions about men and women's roles, but asking for her help with anything, especially a potentially emotional situation, was still difficult. He had no problem offering his own help or even in demanding that she accept it. In that respect they were very much alike—they both had too much pride for their own good.

"I thought it would be better if we told them together," Andy continued. "Not that there'll be any problem or anything, but . . ." He broke off, looking uncomfortable. "If you'd rather not—"

"Of course I'll go," Meg said.

Andy's relief was evident but quickly hidden. "Mom'll be glad to see you."

Meg wished she could return the sentiment. Andy's parents had never been her favorite people. His father she didn't feel as if she had ever known. His mother was so different from her own, different from any woman Meg had ever admired.

On the drive to the Baskins' home, Meg tried to remember the last time she had visited them. It had been before the divorce, of course, perhaps at Christmas eight years ago. Their neighborhood hadn't changed appreciably since then. Located in the Decatur area of the Atlanta metropolitan sprawl, the streets were lined with trees. The homes were ranchers mostly, twenty or thirty years old, much like the house Andy had bought for himself. Though there were some signs of urban decay, for the most part it was still a pleasant area, where children rode their bikes and home owners worked on their lawns.

Andy pulled his car to a stop in the driveway of a brick-and-frame home at the end of a cul-de-sac. Meg noticed the shutters were now painted green instead of white, and the big oak tree that had shaded the front yard was now only a stump.

"Lightning," Andy explained when she asked what had happened. "Good thing it missed the house when it fell. I'm afraid it would have split the place in two."

Privately Meg thought the Baskin home had been split in two many years ago. For surely the members of this family hadn't always been so divided, so ill at ease with one another.

Andy nodded toward the house. "There's Mom on the porch. I guess she was watching for me."

"You must not get over here very often."

His expression guilty, he nodded and returned his mother's wave. Then he took Meg's hand and squeezed it. "I hope this isn't too uncomfortable for you."

His concern touched her. She returned the pressure of his fingers. "I'll survive, Andy."

As they started up the driveway to the front porch, Meg caught Lucy Baskin's momentary surprise at seeing her. It was quickly masked, however.

In her usual fluttering manner, Lucy said, "It's been so long, Meg. Too long. My, but don't you look pretty."

"So do you," Meg returned, meaning the compliment. Mrs. Baskin had always been an attractive woman. Her hair, once the same dark honey as Andy's, was graying, but her blue eyes were still bright, and in her trim yellow slacks and matching blouse, her figure was still slender. Her laughter was the same, also, too high, too frequent. There was a question Meg knew wouldn't be asked in the glance Lucy flashed between her son and his ex-wife.

"Karl," Lucy called as she opened the door. "Look who's with Andy."

A newspaper clutched in one hand, Karl Baskin came into the living room from the direction of the den. He was heavier than Meg remembered, his hair thinner, but basically he was still the same. Upon seeing Meg, he stopped and cleared his throat.

"Dad," Andy said, a trace of irritation in his voice. "It's Meg."

"Well, so it is," Karl answered. His lips quirked at the corners, his version of a smile—or a frown. Meg had always been hard-pressed to tell the difference. Politely he asked, "How are you?"

Lucy answered for Meg. "Well, of course she's fine. She looks fine, doesn't she? You're so slim, Meg. I guess you work out at a gym or something. I need to, but..."

While Lucy chattered on, Meg looked helplessly at Andy and fought hard to suppress a grin.

"Mom," he said, gesturing for his mother to stop. "Mom there's something that I...well, that Meg and I want to tell you." He sounded nervous, so for reassurance, Meg slipped her hand into his again. Lucy's gaze slipped to their joined hands, but she still didn't ask the question that seemed to tremble on her lips. The only sound that disturbed the expectant silence was the faint crackle of Karl's newspaper.

Then Andy told them about the baby. Bluntly. Without preamble.

The roof didn't fall in. It was only after the first awkward moments had passed that Meg realized she had been expecting a dramatic upheaval. But there was nothing of the sort. His father raised an eyebrow. His mother drew in a breath. But that was it. Whatever emotions the announcement might have stirred were hidden.

"Well," Lucy said. "Does this mean you're getting remarried?"

Andy shook his head. "We're just having a baby." His face had taken on the familiar, shuttered expression Meg remembered so well from other visits to his parents' house.

"Well." His mother's voice rose to a squeaky pitch. "Well, my goodness."

"Maybe we should all sit down and talk," Andy suggested.

Lucy turned, nodding. "Let's go in the den. Meg, I'm sure you haven't been here since we've redecorated. You'll see..."

Feeling as if she were caught in some surreal film, Meg followed Andy's mother. Lucy was chattering for all the world as if her son had announced he was going steady, instead of having a baby with a woman who wasn't his wife. Lucy pointed out new upholstery and draperies. Karl sat down in a recliner, not even bothering to switch off the television, where a baseball game was blaring. And then there was Andy. Poor Andy, Meg thought. He stood in the doorway, his mouth drawn tight, his blue eyes dark with resentment.

"Excuse me," he said, breaking into his mother's discourse. "But Meg and I are having a child. Mom, Dad, don't you have anything to say?"

His father cleared his throat, cleared it again, but said nothing. Meg watched him in astonishment. Didn't he feel anything about this? Was he angry, happy, embarrassed?

Andy turned to his mother. "Well?"

"Son, I'm..." Her hand fluttered to her hair and back to her hips, where she nervously pulled at the hem of her blouse. "I guess I'm too surprised to know what to say." She looked at Meg. "The two of you seem happy about this."

Meg stepped forward, touching Lucy's arm. "We're very happy. We hope you will be, too."

Andy said, "Dad, you still haven't said anything."

Karl looked up, not seeming to know what was expected of him. "If you're happy, son..."

It was a feeble answer and not at all what Andy wanted. That much was evident from the way he continued to glare at his father, the way his hands clenched into fists at his sides. Meg wanted him to confront Karl, to demand a reaction. But he didn't. He just stood in the doorway, shifting his weight from foot to foot. Very precisely, Karl folded his newspaper.

Lucy made a soft sound. Meg thought it closer to a sob than a laugh, but it was hard to tell since the older woman was still smiling. A smile so hard and so bright, it was distorted, reminding Meg of a Halloween mask.

It didn't slip as she said, "Andy, you and Meg have a seat. I'm going to go get us something cool to drink. We need..." Lucy's voice broke again. "I'll be right..."

Of the two options presented to Meg—staying in the room with two men who seemed locked in a silent battle of wills or following Lucy to the kitchen—the latter seemed the least objectionable.

She pushed through the swinging door and into the kitchen. "Please let me help...." The words died when she saw Andy's mother, eyes closed, holding on to the edge of the counter as if she would fall to the floor if she let go. "Lucy?"

The older woman jumped. "Oh...oh, my, Meg. I was just...uh...here, let me..." With quick, jerky moments she moved across the kitchen toward the refrigerator.

"It's okay," Meg told her. "It's okay if you're mad about this. Don't be afraid—"

"Mad?" Lucy chirped. "I'm not mad."

Suddenly tired of the facade this woman seemed so intent on projecting, Meg's voice rose. "Then what are you? I mean, it doesn't matter so much to me, but I think Andy would like some kind of reaction from you."

Like a soldier who has stood too long at attention, Lucy seemed to crumple. Slowly she sat in a chair at the kitchen table. "I'm sorry," she whispered. "I shouldn't have run in here like this. But I couldn't stand it."

"You can't stand it about the baby?"

Lucy looked up, aghast. "Oh, no, Meg," she said. "The baby, well, I'm surprised, but..." A smile, a genuine smile, broke across her face. "If you and Andy are happy about it, then I'm thrilled. I'll grant you, the circumstances aren't exactly what I'd expect, but heaven knows, your generation looks at things like this differently. And you and Andy are adults, you don't need my approval."

"But Andy wants it. Why couldn't you tell him you were happy?"

Lucy bit her lip. "I should have, I know. I started to. But then Karl just sat there. And there was Andy, the same as he always is, needing something from his father, something Karl can't seem to give." Tears filled her eyes. "I couldn't stand it."

Meg crossed to the table and put an arm around Lucy's shoulders. "What is it with Andy and his father, anyway?"

"It isn't that Karl doesn't care," Lucy said as she patted Meg's hand.

"Then why does he treat Andy that way?"

"It's the way he is. Karl was always reserved. And then..." She bowed her head.

"Then what?" Meg prompted, although she thought she already knew the answer.

Lucy took a deep breath. "Then David was killed. After that, Karl closed up, especially with Andy. I tried to make it up to Andy, but he wanted his dad's approval—or disapproval...."

"In other words, he wanted his attention." Just like today, Meg thought. Her sympathy then extended to include Andy's mother. She couldn't imagine what it was like to live with a man like Karl. But then again, maybe she could. For in his own way, Andy was as hard to reach as his father. "I don't know how you've stayed married to Karl," she murmured.

"Oh, Meg." A faint smile touched Lucy's mouth again. "Karl's been a good husband, a good provider. We've had a good life together. But when you lose a child…" She shook her head. "The whole world changes when you lose a child."

Meg started to remind the woman that she hadn't lost both her sons, that twenty years was a long time to live in limbo. But she reconsidered. She had never been told the exact circumstances surrounding David's death, only that he'd been caught in the cross fire at a convenience store holdup gone awry. Andy had explained that much, adding that he had decided to go into law enforcement because of the incident. Meg had surmised he felt somehow responsible for his brother's death. Why, she couldn't imagine. He'd been only eleven or twelve. Her attempts to discuss David with him had met with little success.

So Meg couldn't pretend to understand exactly what this family had gone through after David died. And she wouldn't presume to judge them. Perhaps they had coped in the only ways available to them at the time—Karl withdrew, Lucy tried to fill in the silence, and Andy…Andy was left with the residuals Meg knew all too well.

"My goodness," Lucy said now, wiping tears from her cheeks with the backs of her hands. "Let's have some lemonade and calm down. We've got a baby to celebrate, after all."

Meg didn't protest. She thought this home could use some celebration. And when it became clear over the next few minutes that Lucy assumed, perhaps naturally, that Meg and Andy were together even though not thinking of marriage, Meg didn't correct her. This didn't seem the day for trying to explain their confused and confusing relationship.

Somehow Meg made it through the next hour or so. Perhaps understandably, Andy didn't seem inclined to linger, and she was more than ready to leave. It distressed Meg to watch the way these people tiptoed around one another. There had to be a way to bridge the gaps between them. Perhaps she could find a way, if only Andy would let her inside.

Andy said his goodbyes and was headed down the driveway to the car when Lucy touched Meg's arm, holding her back. "About the way I behaved before," the older woman explained, looking embarrassed. "I'm sorry, Meg. I didn't mean to put my troubles onto you."

Meg squeezed her hand. "It's okay. This whole family would be better off if they would share their troubles."

Lucy managed a slight smile. "I'm glad you and Andy are together again. I always thought you were good for him, that he was happier... safer with you."

Safer? The woman's insightful choice of words surprised Meg. Years ago, she had dismissed Lucy Baskin as a silly, vague sort of woman, out of touch with the real world, certainly out of touch with her son. But now Meg realized Lucy knew her son very well. She knew Andy had once lived his life as if it didn't matter when or how it ended.

He says he's changed, Meg told herself as she got into the car and waved goodbye to Lucy. *He says he has more to live for now.* But he was still a cop. A cop who took chances in a city with a soaring crime rate. The thought made her shiver.

"Yeah, I know," Andy muttered. "My parents make you cringe. I'm sorry—"

"It's okay. It wasn't that horrible."

Looking unconvinced, he spared a glance from the road for her. "What did Mom say to you back there?"

"Just that you were safer with me."

"Safer with you?" With a slight laugh, he shook his head. "I guess that means she doesn't understand that we're not really a couple."

"I thought we had hit her with enough bad news for one day."

He nodded. "I'll talk to her, explain the situation."

"She'll probably be disappointed."

"Only because she always thought you'd be able to talk me out of being a cop. Eleven years on the force, and she still hasn't accepted what I do. I think Mom worries more about me being in danger than you ever did."

Remembering the nights she had paced the floor and jumped every time the phone rang, Meg murmured, "I doubt that." She studied Andy's profile for a minute. "Why are you a cop, anyway?"

"What?"

"I really want to know. Why do you do it?"

"You know the answer," he said, flashing his trademark grin. "I seek justice and truth."

His flippancy annoyed her. "I asked you a serious question. I'd appreciate an answer."

"What brought this on?"

She decided on the complete truth. "Your mother and I were talking about David—"

"David?" He sounded startled. "What docs David have to do with anything?"

"You tell me."

"Oh, Meg—"

"Oh, Andy," she said, mocking his tone. "Don't you think it's odd that I've known you all this time and I still don't know what happened to your brother?"

"You do know."

"The bare facts, yes."

"The details don't make for fun conversation."

"I'm not asking to be entertained."

"And I don't want to talk about it." The statement was Andy's standard reply when anyone stepped too close.

Meg wasn't going to accept it this time, as she had for years. Today she had witnessed what could happen to a family that didn't confront their feelings, a family that skirted around delicate issues. She didn't want that for her child. They were going to be an unconventional family as it was. They didn't need other problems. But if Andy couldn't open up to his parents or to her, how would he relate to their child? If Meg pushed hard enough, she thought she might finally begin to understand him. And that understanding might someday help their child.

She didn't push then, however. She would wait until Andy's defenses weren't snapped so firmly in place. And she didn't want to part like this, either, with Andy sullen and resentful. So, impulsively, she invited him to dinner. Though reluctant at first, he stayed and soon began to relax. The evening progressed much as many they had recently spent together. Pleasant. Almost too enjoyable, she thought at one point. Too much like similar, intimate evenings they had shared in the past—before they had decided to behave like grown-ups.

Andy kept telling himself he needed to leave, that the best thing for his sanity was to put a little distance between himself and Meg. But it was too easy to stay. Hell, he wanted to stay. Sitting on her comfortable couch, sipping an after-dinner cup of coffee—decaffeinated, of course—he could almost trick himself into believing they were just any other couple spending a quiet Saturday night at home.

Home. Andy closed his eyes, imagining this was his home, his and Meg's. She had turned the radio to an oldies station. From the kitchen, her singing harmonized in an off-key but thoroughly pleasant way. He smiled, remembering the way she had always sung in the shower and they way he had always laughed at her.

God, how they had laughed. There might have been anger in their past, but they had matched it with laughter.

What were the differences that had driven them apart eight years ago, anyway? He had to concentrate to remember. His job? The thought brought to mind the conversation Meg had tried to begin this afternoon. But Andy pushed that thought aside. He wasn't going to think of pain or problems when he felt so good, when Meg was so near. Tonight he wanted to laugh with her. No, he admitted. He wanted more than laughter. There had been times in the not-so-distant past when the laughter had led to more. So much more.

Setting his coffee mug aside, he went into the kitchen. Meg was at the refrigerator, putting away leftover grilled chicken while she sang about boardwalks and blankets down by the sea. Her hips, shapely even beneath her loose dress, swayed in time to the music.

He caught her around the waist, spinning her into his arms, kicking the refrigerator door shut with his foot.

"Andy, what are you doing?"

"Dancing," he cooed into the silky, fragrant hair above her ear. "Can't you tell dancing when it happens to you?"

She laughed and followed his less-than-expert footwork. "Your dancing is about as good as my singing."

"Think so?" With a flourish, he dipped her. Their bodies pressed close. Their lips were only inches apart. He swung her back to her feet, but she was still only a whisper away. If he moved forward... Knowing he was going way too fast, Andy caught himself, then drew her close as the music on the radio changed to another, even slower song.

Meg resisted his movements. "We shouldn't be dancing," she said softly.

"You need the exercise."

"But Andy—"

"Just dance," he commanded. "The baby wants to dance."

Sighing, she laid her head against his shoulder, and her steps began to follow his. His arms tightened around her so that finally they weren't moving with the music at all, but merely standing still, swaying together. Her body felt full and ripe against his, her breasts pillowing against his chest, her belly nudging his groin. He stirred, hardened in response.

"Andy, stop," Meg said, drawing away. "It's crazy to be doing this."

"Then be crazy."

"Being crazy is what we agreed we wouldn't do."

"We're just dancing," he insisted in his most innocent tones. "We can't waste this music, can we?"

"The music is the same on this station every night."

"But the next time I feel like dancing, your stomach may be too big for me to get my arms around you."

"Andy!"

He pulled her back into his arms. "Just dance, Meg. Don't think about what it could lead to. Just hold me. Let me hold you. That's all I want to do."

Though wariness still darkened her eyes, she acquiesced. And again they swayed together. The music changed time and again, but their steps never altered. Andy closed his eyes, blocking out everything but the feel of Meg in his arms and the not-so-steady pounding of his own heart.

"It isn't fair," he finally declared, breaking the silence. "It's not fair that no one but you ever made me feel this way."

She lifted her head from his shoulder. "That's not true. There have been lots of other women in your life, Andy Baskin."

"But no one like you," he insisted. His lips dipped close to hers once more. "When it comes right down to it, there's only one person I've ever wanted. And baby..." He smiled. "It's you." Then his lips covered hers.

It wasn't until Andy kissed her that Meg realized how much she wanted the touch of his mouth against her own. As he kissed her, the want was identified and intensified. The want became a need. Then a hunger. Greedily she clung to him, her lips parting beneath the pressure of his.

Her arms went around him, hands sliding up his well-muscled back. She breathed in the scent of him, accepted the pressure of his leg as it snaked between her own. Moaning in protest as his mouth left hers, she ground her pelvis downward.

"Meg . . . oh, Meggy."

The sound of Andy's voice, husky and nearly out of control, was what snapped her back to reality. Meg's eyes flew open, and she tried to step back. Only she couldn't. Andy had conveniently backed her into the corner formed by her kitchen cabinets.

His hands slipped up her bare arms. "You're so sweet. I always forget how sweet . . ." His mouth lowered toward hers again, but she dodged him.

"Andy, let me go," she said, pushing against his chest.

Now his eyes opened. He seemed to have trouble focusing them. "What?"

This time when Meg pushed, she succeeded in putting some distance between the two of them. "We weren't going to do this. Remember?"

Hands going to her shoulders, he said, "I'd rather forget."

She shrugged him off. "You tricked me, Andy."

That got his attention. "Why do you say that?"

"The dancing. The sweet nothings in my ear."

"I happened to have meant those sweet nothings."

"You always mean them, don't you?" She started toward the sun room. "Especially when a piece of your anatomy other than your brain is in control."

He caught her arm and hauled her around to face him. He wasn't laughing now. "Wait a minute, Meg. I was telling the truth when I said no one but you has ever made me feel so . . . so . . ." He struggled for the right word.

"Hard?" Meg supplied, ice in her voice.

"That's not it at all."

She glanced down to the fly of his shorts, raised an eyebrow and looked up at him again. "Really?"

"Oh, dammit," he muttered. "This isn't just about sex."

"I don't know what else you'd call this...this thing between us."

He caught her hands in his. "It's passion, yes. But it's a helluva lot more. I mean, haven't you felt differently the last few weeks? We've been close, the way we should have been years ago."

His words tugged at her heart. He was right. In many respects, they had never been closer. Yet still there was this distance. "It isn't enough," she insisted. "And I'm not settling for half measures ever again, especially not when there's a baby involved. I won't get on this roller coaster ride with you again, Andy. Up one day. Miserable the next. It isn't the way to raise a child." She pulled her hands from his grasp. "Now we've made a promise—"

"I'd like to renegotiate."

"Forget it." She started to walk away.

"We could try to make it work, you know, before the baby gets here."

She wheeled to face him. "Andy, I don't want to play house. Especially with a man who can't share anything more than sex with me."

Face flushing, he stiffened. "I don't know how you can say that. You know I'm not the same as I was before. For the last few weeks, I've been here for you. Right now, I'd do anything for you, for our child."

"Would you?" Eyes narrowing, Meg stepped close to him again. "Then share something with me, Andy. Tell me about David."

He sucked in his breath. "Why is David so damn important to you?"

"Because he was important to you," she said, anger making her voice shake. "Because whatever happened to David helped make you the person you are now. And that person is the father of my child."

Andy turned away from her. "David died a long time ago. Sometimes I can't even remember..." He paused. "Sometimes I don't remember his face."

Meg knew he was lying. She could hear it in his voice. "Isn't David's death the reason you're a cop? Aren't you trying to right some kind of wrong?"

He shook his head and lifted his gaze toward the ceiling. "Maybe. I don't know. Maybe seeing your brother get blown away—"

"Wait a minute," Meg interrupted, feeling the blood drain from her face. "You saw him die?"

Andy wouldn't look at her. "I don't want to talk about this, Meg. I don't know why that makes me some kind of freak."

"It doesn't—"

"Then let it alone," he said, turning on her again. "Please just let this alone!"

"But I want to understand."

"Okay. Then understand," he shouted. "David died for me. He took the bullet for me, all right? Are you satisfied now? Do you understand what makes me tick?"

The fury in his face made Meg press a hand to her mouth. She closed her eyes, imagining all sorts of horrors. Too much horror for any little boy to endure. Her chest was aching when she opened her eyes again.

But Andy was gone.

The slam of the front door told her she had pushed too hard this time.

Chapter Six

Years ago, when Andy and Meg quarreled, she was the one who ran away. He always followed, eager to make up, to convince her everything was all right. It worked for almost two years. And even after their divorce, when they would see each other and let passion rule, he always came after her when it was over. To no avail, of course, but he would call her for a while, anyway, as if he thought it was expected of him. Pursuer and pursuee. Those were the roles they had assumed from the beginning.

But now it was Meg's turn to run to Andy.

Nearly a week had passed since the night he had left her condo, a week in which Meg had answered every phone call, expecting the caller would be him. A week in which she had spent most of her time berating herself over pushing him so hard.

At work she was short-tempered and distracted. Her colleagues, who were still in shock over her pregnancy announcement, avoided her. At home she was restless and lonely. She had complained to Perri about having Andy around all the time. Now she missed him. And sometimes, when she thought about having the baby without him around, she was overwhelmed by anxiety and fear. Yes, fear, from a woman who only weeks ago had been proclaiming she could do everything on her own. The degree to which she missed him was both unsettling and dangerous to her emotional health.

At the same time, she *had* to see him.

Waiting until the usual snarl of Friday afternoon traffic cleared, she drove from her office to his place. But Andy wasn't alone. A red sports car and a blue Bronco were parked in the driveway. As Meg let her car pause in the street, a small blond-haired boy got out of the latter vehicle and raced around the side of the house, but the woman getting out of the driver's side—Lisa—turned and looked straight at Meg. Though Meg would have liked nothing better than to speed away, she was caught. So she pulled into the driveway and got out.

Shifting the grocery bag she carried to one hip, Lisa walked toward her. "Andy didn't say you were coming, Meg."

Nervously Meg fiddled with the strap of her purse. "He doesn't know. I...uh...I wanted to talk to him. I didn't know he was having anyone over."

"Oh." Lisa studied Meg intently for a moment. "Listen, Meg, this may be none of my business, but I happen to care a lot about Andy—"

"I know," Meg said, nodding. "He says you're his best friend."

"He helped me through some hard times."

"I'm sure you've done the same for him."

"And I'm sure you, of all people, understand when I say getting Andy to accept any kind of help isn't easy."

"That's the understatement of the century." The two women laughed together, and some of the tension eased from Meg.

"Like I said," Lisa continued. "This may be none of my business, but Andy's been really uptight the times we've talked or seen each other this week. And that bothered me, considering that during the last few weeks he's been so high, so excited about the baby...."

"So you know about the baby," Meg said, even though she wasn't surprised.

Brown paper crackled as Lisa shifted her grocery sack again. "I also know that you two were getting along fine. And now Andy is walking around looking as if his world has caved in. It reminds me of how he acted when you decided you wanted a divorce."

"We decided that together," Meg corrected.

Lisa paused for a moment, one smooth eyebrow arching, as if she didn't believe Meg. "Well, whatever," she said finally. "The only thing I have to say is that Andy wants to be a good father to your child. I hope the two of you can work out whatever it is that's happened." Her smile was tentative. "I hope you don't mind me speaking frankly...."

"No, of course not." Meg took a deep breath. "I appreciate your concern. In fact, I'd like us to be friends. You're so close to Andy. And sometimes...most of the time, I don't understand him at all. That's what this—" She broke off as a shout rang out from the side of the house.

"Hey, Lisa!" Andy called as he rounded the corner near the garage doors. "Are we having burgers or are you—" He stopped when his gaze connected with Meg's.

Lisa stepped back. "I'm going inside to make hamburger patties right now, Hotshot." She smiled at Meg. "I hope you'll be sticking around for dinner."

Meg waited until the other woman had disappeared before speaking. Squaring her shoulders, she walked toward Andy. "I guess you're surprised to see me."

He hooked thumbs in the belt loops of his cutoffs and looked toward the street, avoiding her eyes. "I guess one of us had to end the stalemate, didn't we?"

"I'm sorry there had to be a stalemate."

"Me, too." He still didn't look at her.

Meg bit her lip. "Most of all, I'm sorry about the other night. I didn't mean to cause you pain, Andy, I just..."

Finally he allowed his gaze to meet hers again. "Maybe it's good that you pushed. Maybe you have some of your answers now."

She didn't, of course. What Andy had told her Saturday night had only raised more questions in her mind. She still wanted to know exactly what had happened when David was killed. She wanted a clear understanding of how the incident continued to influence Andy's life. But she knew those answers would come only when Andy was ready to give them. "I shouldn't have been so pushy," she repeated.

"That just seems to come naturally to you."

"I know sometimes I'm impatient."

"Impatient? That's a mild term for it."

She bristled at his scoffing tone. "You're not exactly the king of forbearance, yourself."

He exhaled deeply. "I don't want to fight with you again, Meg."

She sighed, refusing to let the anger that had sparked inside her take hold. "Same here."

"Let's forget what happened the other night."

Which part of what happened? she wondered. The argument or what had come before—the way he had touched her, kissed her. Deliberately she closed her mind to the memory of those kisses. Even more than their fight, the feel of his mouth moving against her own had haunted her all this week. And she refused to give in to that memory now or ever again.

"It's forgotten," she said, holding her hand out to Andy.

He didn't shake her hand. He stared at it for a moment, then looked at her, an inscrutable expression in his blue eyes, and he thrust his hands into his pockets. Awkwardly she let her arm swing back to her side.

Andy jerked his head toward the back of the house. "Lisa and her son and my partner, Will Espinoza, are going to have dinner here. You're welcome to stay, if you'd like."

Meg was sure he expected her to refuse. When they were married, she hadn't liked being around his friends who were on the force. Maybe it was because they, like any other group of co-workers, tended to talk shop, and she feared what they seemed to make so light of. Maybe she resented how much he shared with them that he wouldn't share with her. However, Meg had decided she didn't want whatever future relationship she had with Andy to be crippled by past fears. So she nodded. "I'd love to stay for dinner."

His surprise was quickly masked as he turned to go back around the house. "Come on. We're eating out on the deck."

Meg was greeted easily by Lisa, who put her to work slicing tomatoes and tearing lettuce. Her son, Terry, an exuberant six-year-old, was friendly but spent most of his time tossing sticks for Boomer to fetch. Andy's new partner was presiding over the grill.

Will Espinoza seemed younger than Andy. At the same time, there was a look in his dark eyes that was very old. Dressed as Andy was in police-department T-shirt and shorts, he was at once approachable and yet reserved. Meg knew Will was aware of her pregnancy, because when he didn't think she was looking, she caught his speculative glance at her still almost flat stomach. She should have known Andy would tell him. Eventually a cop shared more with his partner than he did with his wife. Will grinned when their eyes met, a tentative smile that softened his chiseled features.

The evening was warm but not uncomfortable, though Meg shed her white linen jacket and wished for a cool pair of shorts like the others were wearing. As the burgers were ready to come off the grill, the sun set in a spectacular showcase of orange and purple on the horizon. Lavender shadows crept over the spacious backyard, and Terry became more interested in chasing lightning bugs than eating. From neighboring houses came the smoky, sizzling meat scent of other Friday night barbecues, the sounds of other children laughing and playing. Andy lit citronella candles and turned on his bug zapper to keep pesky insects at bay. And Meg found herself enjoying the evening, even though Andy had little to say to her.

In between pleas for her son to come and eat, Lisa kept up a lively debate with Will. The two seemed to disagree on everything, from the president's economic policy to the latest box office smash. The tension between the two of them was palpable. And sexual, Meg thought, smiling a bit as she listened to them.

When their debate over a popular television detective series threatened to escalate into a full-scale argument, Meg spoke before thinking. "My goodness,

you two, you sound just like Andy and I used to. And
you know how that..." She stopped, realizing what
she might be implying by her remark.

Dead silence followed. Lisa stared at her, Will
looked uncomfortable, and Andy's mouth thinned
into a stern line. Meg didn't quite understand his anger. She had put her foot in her mouth, true, but was
it really any reason to become angry? He pushed his
chair away from the umbrellaed table. "How about
another beer—Lisa, Will?" Not waiting for their replies, he went into the house.

Still confused about why her remark had so bothered Andy, Meg cleared her throat. "I didn't mean...I
wasn't implying..." She broke off, realizing her explanation was making everyone more uncomfortable.
She stood. "Why don't I clear the table?"

Lisa got up also. "Good idea."

Soon Andy came back outside with three beers, and
the awkward moment passed. Will and Lisa stopped
arguing, and perhaps inevitably, the talk turned to
police work, in particular a murder investigation Andy
and Will had recently closed.

"The man is amazing," Will said, turning to Meg.
"I was told before being assigned to him what to expect, but I didn't believe it at first. He doesn't miss a
thing."

Andy looked embarrassed. "Oh, come on, Espinoza. You would have wrapped the case up, even
without me."

Will shrugged. "Maybe, but not as fast."

"What happened?" Meg asked.

"We had a three-days-dead body," Will replied bluntly. "And no witnesses. The man's house had been ransacked, so the motive was pretty clear. But there were no suspects. Very few clear fingerprints other than the victim's. I mean, neighbors on all four sides said they saw nothing. The guy was an old man, in ill health, a loner. But his nephew said he used to keep a lot of cash on hand. We didn't find much on the premises."

Meg leaned forward, intrigued despite herself. "What broke the case?"

"Nothing gets by Andy," Will said, shaking his head. "When we were talking to neighbors, he noticed this kid riding this brand-new bicycle. The boy was about fourteen or so. He kept riding up and down the street while we went from house to house. I didn't think much of it, but Andy did. Some neighborhood kids told us the boy's name. He lived a couple of streets over. And from the looks of his family's house, their budget didn't run to new bicycles."

Horrified, Meg put a hand to her throat. "This kid killed an old man for the money to buy a bicycle?"

"It appears that way. He confessed."

"How did you know?" Meg asked Andy.

He took a swig of his beer and shrugged. "Just a hunch. I saw the kid on that new bike and thought it looked out of place. But I knew something was up when I asked the boy's mother about the bike. I mean, the woman didn't have to tell me anything. But she was nervous. Finally she said she was afraid her son was mixed up with drug dealers and that was how he had bought the bike." He stopped, pensively studying his beer again. "She's a good person, that kid's mother. She has too many children, a drunk for a husband and a lousy job, but she's trying. Running drugs isn't what she wants for her kid. She asked us to talk to him."

"But I don't think she expected him to confess to murder," Will muttered.

Andy nodded. "He says he never intended to murder the guy. He heard the old guy had money stashed. He broke in. The man resisted. You can fill in the rest."

Sitting back in her chair, Meg said, "I wonder why the kid kept riding up and down the street like that."

"Because he hadn't yet developed the instincts of a full-fledged criminal," Lisa said. "He didn't know he shouldn't return to the scene of the crime. And he certainly wasn't aware of the famous Andy Baskin instincts."

"Hardly famous," Andy retorted.

"No, just legendary." Will tipped his beer bottle in Andy's direction. "You finally made a believer out of me, *amigo.*"

Andy got up abruptly, calling to Terry and Boomer. Meg could see how embarrassed he was. But his discomfort and protests only urged Lisa and Will on. They began recounting stories of Andy's successes. He had tangled with drug dealers and street gangs, had come through in tense moments on domestic disturbance calls and responded with speed and bravery to officers in trouble codes. It was obvious how much he was respected by these officers and, no doubt, by others on the force.

Though she knew Andy was dedicated to his job, knew he was a good cop, Meg had never seen the esteem in which he was held. She had been so busy worrying about him, she hadn't bothered to look at what he did from any perspective other than her own. Knowing his father's indifference and his mother's fears, she wondered if anyone other than these people had ever expressed any pride in what he did. The thought made her uncomfortable, made her feel terribly selfish.

When his fellow officers had badgered him for a while, Andy returned to his chair, crossed his arms and glared at Lisa. "All this talk about my famous instinct is a setup, Lisa. You want me to tell you to trust *your* instincts on the arson case you've been working on. You know, the case you keep thinking is murder, when it was really a terrible, tragic accident."

Lisa sniffed. "You aren't the only one who can play out a hunch, Lieutenant Hotshot. I'm going to prove there was a murder."

"We'll see, won't we?"

With that, Andy turned the conversation to other topics. Terry and Boomer finally left the yard and came to rest on the deck, the dog at Andy's feet, the boy in his lap.

From what Meg had seen tonight, Terry was a fiercely independent child, and he was far from a baby. So it said something about the ease of his and Andy's relationship that he could climb into the man's lap and go to sleep. Watching them warmed Meg's heart. She found herself fantasizing about other such scenes between Andy and their own child.

The yearning left her feeling melancholy. She lingered while Andy carried Terry to the car and said goodbye to Lisa and Will. When he didn't immediately return, she decided to make herself useful and went into the kitchen. Boomer followed her and sat down in the center of the room, his eyes watching her every movement as she tossed paper plates into the trash and rinsed silverware in preparation for the dishwasher. He whined when she started to wrap the leftover hamburgers in plastic.

"Didn't you have enough burgers before?" she asked the dog. "You ate Terry's."

Boomer barked in response. And playing the game she and the dog had perfected years ago, Meg held a meat patty high off the floor. Boomer leaped on hind legs and snatched it from her fingers. She laughed in delight.

From the kitchen doorway, Andy devoured the sight of Meg's pretty, animated features as she knelt and hugged his pet. He wished he didn't react as he did to her presence. He didn't want to want her. It was a desire he was going to have to get over once and for all.

In the days since he had run out on her, he had come to some hard realizations about their relationship. Meg was being sensible when she said the baby was all they could ever share. He knew now he was never going to wheedle or talk his way into sharing her bed or her life. In fact, he didn't want to share them. At least not by those means.

Meg wanted something he would never be able to give. Oh, it wasn't just her questions about his brother's death that he couldn't answer. What she needed from him went deeper, much deeper. It had to do with really being a part of each other's lives. Maybe he had too much of his father in him to let anyone else in. No matter how much or how often he told himself he wanted genuine closeness, he didn't think he could do it. Not to the degree that Meg seemed to desire, anyway. He had known that about himself for quite a while. He could try, but he had a feeling he would always fall short of her expectations. And if he pretended, it would only break Meg's heart.

And his.

Again.

Meg looked up, saw him, and her smile deepened. Andy had to look away. It was strange how a smile like that could cut your insides as sharply as a frown.

"You don't have to clean up," he said gruffly as he crossed to the sink. "I know it's late and you've probably had a long day."

She straightened. "No longer than most."

He opened the dishwasher's door and began loading knives and forks inside. "You feeling okay?"

"A little more morning sickness. Nothing major."

"Good." He closed the dishwasher with a little bang and grabbed a damp sponge from the back of the sink. "I'm going out to clean off the grill, so . . ."

"Andy?"

He looked at her, really met her gaze for the first time since they had talked in the driveway when she arrived. "Is there something you want to talk about?"

She fiddled with the waistband of her skirt, touched her stomach, a nervous gesture he had seen her make several times tonight. "Are we going to be like this from now on?" she asked.

"Like what?"

"Like polite strangers."

He rubbed his jaw. "I'm sorry, Meg, but..." Somehow, he couldn't fit his feelings into any of the words that came to mind.

"You probably won't believe this," she said, her dark eyes solemn as she stepped forward. "But I missed you this week." Lightly she touched his arm.

He jerked away. Anger snapped inside him. "Don't do that."

"But Andy, I—"

"You can't have it both ways," he bit out. "You can't tell me you don't want to play house while you keep up the same old flirtatious games."

"This isn't a game."

"Isn't it?" He turned around, tossing the sponge into the sink, bracing his arms on the edge of the counter while he stared through the window at the darkened backyard. Reflected in the glass, he saw Meg come to stand beside him. Some of his irritation eased. "Maybe you aren't playing games," he muttered. "Maybe the whole problem is mine."

"Andy, what are you talking about?"

He looked at her. "You were right the other night, you know, after I kissed you. You said I tricked you, and you were right."

"I don't think I was really serious about that accusation."

"You should have been." He shook his head. "Ever since this whole thing happened, you've been saying we had to stop falling into the same old patterns. I kept agreeing with you, but my heart wasn't in it. You see..." He stopped and gave a mirthless laugh, feeling foolish. Then he plunged on, "You see, I want you, Meg."

Flushing, she looked away. "I know that, Andy."

"No," he said. "No, you don't know, Meg. You don't know how much I want you, how often over the past few weeks I've tried to let myself believe that wanting you is enough, that things could be right between us."

She lifted her chin and faced him again. "What do you mean by right?"

"The way they should be between two people who are bringing a child into the world."

For a moment there was silence, then she asked, "What should we do about it?"

"Nothing." He turned back to the window, unable to look into her dark eyes any longer. "I can stop tricking you. Or wishing. There's nothing I can do, because it won't ever be right between us."

She said nothing.

"No matter how much I pretend," Andy continued, trying to convince himself as much as her. "It won't be right. We proved we couldn't do that a long time ago. I have to keep reminding myself. I have to accept it. I mean, *really* accept it. I hadn't done that until this week.''

Meg knew she should feel relieved. Andy was accepting what she had known to be the truth for a long time. There would be no more foolishness between them, no more dancing in the kitchen, no more kisses. He would stop being flirtatious. He would give her some space. That was what she had told Perri she wanted, wasn't it? So why, instead of relief, did she have this big hollow feeling inside?

''It's funny, you know,'' he said in a quiet voice. ''We've been divorced for a long time, but I believe I always thought we'd eventually work it out. I kept waiting, thinking…yeah, me and Meg, someday we'll find the magic formula for happiness.'' He shrugged. ''I guess I believed the baby was going to be that magic.'' He looked up at her, his eyes deep, troubled wells. ''I was wrong.''

Wrong. The word resonated through her till she wanted to scream. Yet again, she had received exactly what she had wished for. So she might as well behave like a good girl and accept this with good graces. ''I'm glad you're being so sensible about this, Andy.''

''It's the only way to be. I see that now.''

With quick movements designed to keep him from seeing how she was trembling, she turned on the water, washed her hands and dried them on a dishcloth. ''I still don't think there's anything to prevent us from being good parents.''

"No."

"And there's no reason we can't finally just be friends."

Their gazes met then, but Andy's skipped away fast. "No reason at all. I'll still be here for you... all through this..." He cleared his throat. "Always."

She didn't want to think about always. Always meant forever being without Andy's touch. Turning on her heel, she went into the dining room and took her jacket from the chair where she had draped it earlier. "My next doctor's appointment is in two weeks. Do you want to go?"

He nodded. "Call and remind me."

"Fine." She picked up her purse and looked at Andy, who stood with Boomer in the kitchen doorway. She felt as if she should be saying, doing something more. But what could she do? Tell him she had changed her mind, that she wanted to play house, wanted him on any basis at all? That was nonsense. And it would be a lie, too, for she wanted much more than that with him. But as he said, they had proven long ago that they couldn't get it right.

So even though it was an effort, she smiled and left.

The same sort of forced civility reigned between them for nearly two months. They saw each other, of course. Andy still called or came by to see how she was feeling. But there was no spontaneity between them now. Very little laughter. No dancing in the kitchen. On the day the baby's movement became something more than the flutter of butterfly wings, Meg forgot herself and tore over to his house after work. They even laughed about it, got excited together. But there was no touching. Very carefully, Andy restrained himself when he seemed to be thinking about touching her.

And that was difficult for Meg. For she wanted Andy to touch her, as she had never wanted it before. As the days sped by, August blending into September and then October, her body seemed to change daily. Her breasts were lusher, tender to the touch. The tiny bump in her stomach had belled forward into a pronounced curve. The sight amazed her when she stood naked in front of her mirror. Sometimes she felt heavy and unattractive, but more often she felt ripe, sexy. She often fantasized about what Andy would think of the differences in her shape.

Fearing that such thoughts made her into some sort of pervert, she confided in Perri, who laughed. "Meg, some of the most astounding sex of my life occurred during the sixth month of my second pregnancy." Flushing under her freckles, Perri confessed, "I was insatiable. Rod was a truly happy man."

But Meg had no one upon whom to bestow the benefits of her sexual feelings. She even thought about inviting Andy over, lighting some candles and greeting him at the door in a black lace gown. But she wasn't sure even that would work. He was so careful not to touch her, not to behave in any manner that she could misconstrue.

So they continued, sharing one of the most joyful experiences a man and a woman can share and yet sharing nothing at all.

Meg began to wonder how much longer she could stand it.

For her October doctor's appointment, a sonogram was schedule. Andy told himself it wasn't going to be any big deal. On a monitor, they would be able to see a picture of the baby, sort of like an X ray. They would see that it was healthy, perhaps tell its gender. He couldn't imagine it would be any more wondrous than the first time he heard the heartbeat.

He was wrong.

When they met in the lobby of the doctor's office building, Meg was more nervous than he had ever seen her. They found seats in a corner of the crowded waiting room, and she whispered, "What if something's wrong, Andy? What should we do?"

He wanted to take her hand, squeeze it tight or perhaps kiss the worried line from between her eyebrows. But such comforts were no longer available to him. "Has there been any reason to expect there to be something wrong?"

"No, but—"

"Then stop worrying."

She twisted her hands together in her lap. "I just keep thinking about how I felt when I realized I was pregnant. For a minute, I didn't want the baby."

He looked at her in surprise. "You never told me that."

"I feel so guilty for ever thinking it."

"But it was only natural."

"I know, and I can understand other women not being happy about being pregnant. But this baby..." She sucked in her breath. "This baby is real to me now."

"So it doesn't matter what you thought in the beginning."

"But now what if something's wrong?"

"You're not making a lot of sense, Meg."

She pressed a hand to her obviously swollen stomach. Andy followed the movement greedily, wishing he could do the same. "I know I'm being crazy," Meg murmured. "Crazy and unreasonable and afraid."

"Then let's not do it."

She shook her head. "We have to. We have to know that she's all right."

"*He* is all right," Andy assured her. "And remember, people have been having healthy babies without sonograms for a lot of years. So we can get up and walk out of here if you want."

"No." She squeezed her eyes shut then opened them again. Her hand groped toward him. "Hold my hand, please. I just want you to hold my hand."

He couldn't refuse a plea like that. He wrapped his fingers around hers, as he had yearned to do from the moment he had seen her strained, tense face. Meg held on for dear life.

Andy was surprised by her reaction to this relatively simple medical procedure. Strong, confident, independent Meg wasn't afraid very often. When they met for the first time, her apartment had just been broken into, but she had been more angry than fearful. And over the years, when she claimed to be afraid for him because of his job, the emotion had seemed more like resentment or fury. Or both. Only twice had he glimpsed real terror in her face. Once, on a February night when she had come to the hospital and found him in Lisa's arms. And again today.

She was very pale as she lay on the examining table. She remained still while her sweater was lifted and the waistband of her skirt rolled down in preparation for the sonogram.

The technician, a pretty young woman who hardly looked old enough to have graduated high school, tried to reassure her. "There's nothing to be frightened about, you know."

Andy patted Meg's hand. "I told you."

Meg nodded but looked unconvinced.

Smiling his encouragement, Andy let his gaze stray to the smooth golden skin of Meg's stomach, on which the technician was spreading a gel. Since their last visit to the doctor a month before, her stomach had grown noticeably. And why not? She was five months pregnant. Five months had passed since that fateful night in May. He glanced at her stomach again. Now it looked as if there was a baby growing inside her.

A few minutes later, when an image popped onto the monitor beside the table, there was no doubt at all.

The feeling that built inside him was like Christmas morning, graduation day and the first time he had kissed Meg—all rolled into one. At the same time, the feeling was like nothing else he had ever known. The image was unmistakably a baby. Stretching. Opening his tiny mouth. Drawing his legs upward. Andy stared at that tiny life in stupefied wonder.

Meg clung even tighter to his hand. "I didn't expect the picture to be so clear."

The technician said, "The technology keeps getting better and better."

"But I see her." Meg laughed in pure delight. "Do you see her, Andy?"

"Yeah." He tore his gaze from the monitor to look down at her. He felt his smile growing broader. "I see him, all right."

"Uh-oh." The young technician laughed. "Sounds as if there's some disagreement as to the gender of this child."

Andy asked, "Shouldn't we be able to tell from this?"

"Well, most of the time..." The young woman frowned as she gazed at the screen.

"What is it?" Meg demanded, fear in her voice.

Startled, Andy looked back at the screen. "Is something wrong?"

"Oh, no, no," the technician assured them. "Nothing's wrong, I was just trying to see if this is a little guy or a little girl. But see the way the legs are drawn up?" She pointed at the screen. "I can't see, but I think..." The baby moved, and she squinted, looking closely. "I think it might be a girl...no...well, it's hard to say with the way the baby is positioned."

"It's not important," Meg said, eyes still riveted on the screen, hand still wrapped in Andy's. "As long as everything is okay."

Andy nodded, entranced by the image on the screen. This was a person, a life he and Meg had created. The baby had been real to him for months now. He had spent countless hours daydreaming about the things he and his son would do together. But this . . . this took his breath away.

The technician smiled. "Everything looks good. I believe your baby is fine."

Good? Fine? Andy wondered how a miracle could be described in such colorless words. Perhaps this woman was jaded by having seen so many babies. But this was his baby. His and Meg's.

He asked, "Can't we watch it for a while?"

"We've videotaped this," the technician said, grinning. "You can take the tape home and watch it as many times as you want. Everyone can see it with you."

With an excited little laugh, Meg squeezed his hand. "Can we have two tapes?"

"You see," Andy began. "We don't . . ." Suddenly the need for two tapes seemed too complicated to explain. "Never mind. I'll make a copy myself."

A moment later, as suddenly as it had appeared, the baby's image was gone from the monitor.

"That's it," the technician said brightly. "See, there was nothing to be frightened about."

Andy grinned at Meg like a totally besotted fool. He couldn't stop smiling. On the ride down in the elevator to the lobby, he almost laughed out loud. The happiness kept unfurling inside him—like a giant multicolored balloon. He thought he would explode from the excitement.

Meg looked equally dazzled. Outside the building, she took his hand and did a little skip as she hugged the tape to her chest. "I don't think I can go back to work," she said, her brown eyes sparkling in the clear October sunshine.

"Who can think about work?"

"Then let's go home. Let's watch the baby again."

He didn't bother to ask which home. He guided her to his car and drove to her condo. And once there, they watched the tape over and over again. Meg sat on the floor, Andy beside her on the edge of the low coffee table in her sun room. Straining toward the television, they exclaimed over every movement the baby made.

"Can you believe us?" Meg finally demanded. "We sound like . . . like parents."

"Goofy, doting parents," Andy agreed. "The kind who bring snapshots of their baby taking a bath to work."

Meg got to her knees, so that she was almost level with him. "We've got to get a grip, Andy. Otherwise, we'll stay this way, and by the time the baby is five years old she'll be so embarrassed and disgusted by our behavior she'll go live with my parents."

"Okay, we'll get a grip."

For a moment there was silence, then Meg said, in a quiet voice, "Wanna watch it again?"

His eyes met hers. He smiled. "Yeah."

They laughed together. And before Meg even recognized her own intent, she reached up and kissed Andy on the cheek. He turned, startled, and then his lips were only a movement away from hers. This time she considered what she was going to do. For half a second, she thought about it. Then she kissed him again.

Andy pulled away. "Meg, we said—"

"I don't care what we said."

"But we shouldn't—"

"The can'ts and the shouldn'ts can all go to hell." She kissed him once more, and in the kiss she put all the joy she had felt today, all the frustration that had pressed in on her for the past few months.

Again Andy pulled back. He touched a hand to her hair. Gently he tucked a tendril behind her ear. "But why, Meg? Why would we do this?"

"Because I want you."

"That isn't—"

"Yes," she cut in, knowing what he was going to say. "Wanting you is the point. At least it is right now." Breath catching on a trembling sigh, she placed her cheek against his shoulder and closed her eyes. "I'm so full, Andy. Full of all these feelings. The only way I can think of expressing them is to make love with you. I don't want to think about it. I just want you to touch me." She looked up at him again. "Touch me like you did the night we made the baby."

Andy knew they were both overcome with emotion, a little high from the experience of actually seeing their child. He didn't want to get carried away with the moment. Although his body tightened at the thought of touching Meg, he couldn't afford to do this. If he made love to her now, he was afraid he would never want to walk away again.

He turned, and Meg's body settled quite naturally between his spread thighs. He framed her earnest, pretty face with his hands. "Tomorrow, you may regret this."

She shrugged. "Maybe. I don't want to worry about that now."

"Then I have to worry."

She placed her fingers against his lips. "Don't. Don't think about it. If we think about it, we'll both get scared. So just love me." Like the whisper of silk, her fingertips stroked across his jaw. "Love me. Please."

And so he kissed her. Gently at first, them with the raw, pent-up emotion of months of denial. She kept pace with the demands of his kiss. She made a few demands of her own. In breathless, gasping whispers. In the urgent touch of her hands on his body. They didn't worry about the niceties. There, on carpet warmed by the October afternoon sun, they threw off the clothes that got in their way.

Then they rocked together. Swung on a star.

Afterward they lay apart, breathing hard.

Andy stared at the ceiling, trying to collect his thoughts. "Well," he said. "That was—"

"Just the beginning," Meg whispered. She pressed close to his side, her hand sliding across his belly, closing over his sex. She grinned at his gasp. "Any chance of a rematch?"

Since Andy was momentarily robbed of the power of speech, he was glad his body could answer for him.

Chapter Seven

The sun had disappeared and been replaced by a big harvest-bright moon when Meg awakened in Andy's arms. Earlier, after it became obvious how they were going to spend the afternoon, she had called her office and cleared the rest of her day. He did the same. He even called a neighbor to take care of Boomer. After exhausting the sun room floor's possibilities, they had moved upstairs to her bedroom. There, in the comfort of her brass bed with its pure cotton sheets, beneath the patchwork quilt her Grandma Kathy had made them as a wedding gift, they had promptly fallen asleep.

Now Meg lay on her side, one hand on her stomach, her gaze on Andy's face. The moonlight slanted through the blinds and highlighted the angular lines of his profile. He looked so at peace. She felt so safe with him here beside her. *Safe?* She frowned at the thought. Feeling safe and secure wasn't something that depended on anyone's presence but her own. So why did Andy's being here suddenly make such a difference?

He stirred before she could find an answer. Stretching in the distinctively masculine way she remembered, he came awake by degrees. Yawning first. Rubbing a hand across his face. Eyes opening. Then that smile. That glorious Andy Baskin smile. He was the only person she had ever known who woke up smiling.

Pushing the covers down his chest, his smile grew broader as he said, "Hi, there."

She turned onto her back and snuggled deeper in the bed, content for the moment. "Hi, yourself."

"Man, this bed is comfortable." He stretched again. "We are the only two people in the world who would spend hours down on the carpet when a bed like this was waiting up here."

She chuckled, blushing a little as she remembered some of the things they had done on that carpet. "I guess we were in a hurry."

"We're not in a hurry now." Sliding down into the covers again, he moved across the bed, his arms bringing her close. He pressed his lips against her bare shoulder and took a deep breath. "Damn, but I've missed the way you smell, Meg."

"The way I smell?"

"I imagine I could pick you out of a crowd of women, just by your scent."

Turning so that she faced him, she said, "It's funny the things you remember, isn't it?"

He propped himself up on one elbow and ever so lightly brushed his fingertips across her face. "I'll always remember today."

She nodded. "It was pretty spectacular."

"The baby . . ." He shook his head. "It was incredible."

Although the baby was spectacular, it wasn't the event to which Meg had been referring. Oddly disappointed, she drew away. "Excuse me, but impending motherhood means a few more trips to the bathroom than usual."

"Sure."

Throwing back the covers, she padded across the darkened room to her bathroom. When she bent over her sink to wash her hands, she looked at her reflection and told herself not to be silly about Andy's remark. Of course the big thing about today was the baby. It was what had drawn them together. But she couldn't help thinking—remembering a time when their lovemaking would have been the most incredible part of the day for Andy. Yes, it was funny what a person remembered. Trying to shake off her disquieting thoughts, she started back to bed.

She had taken two steps into the room when Andy said, "Don't move."

In the light that streamed from the bathroom, she could just make out his form in the bed. "What is it?"

"Stand right there."

"Andy, it's cold."

"But you look so perfect." He scrambled out of bed and came toward her. "With the light at your back and the mirror in front of you..."

Only then did Meg realize she had paused in front of the full-length, brass-framed mirror that stood outside the bathroom door. She took a step backward.

Andy gently nudged her forward again. Standing behind her, with his hands on her shoulders, he met her gaze in the mirror. "You look so beautiful." His fingers stroked down her arms, raising goose bumps in their wake. "Like a Greek statue."

For the first time that day, Meg felt shy over the changes that had occurred in her body. She had been naked with Andy so many times, she hadn't thought to be modest this afternoon. She had wanted him so much, she had simply enjoyed the way he touched her, the feelings he had aroused. But now, with his gaze passing over her with the slow sweetness of warm honey, she flushed and put a hand on the curve of her stomach. "I guess my shape looks classical," she conceded. "They liked their women voluptuous, didn't they?"

Instead of answering her, he leaned forward, kissing one side of her neck. His breath was warm on her skin. He moved close behind her, so close she could feel the velvety length of his sex stirring against her, so close the heat of his body warmed her through and through. In the mirror, she watched his hands slip from her arms to her belly and then up to her breasts. A delicious, languid ache began there and spread downward.

Her breath came out in a slow, heavy sigh. Arching back against him, she closed her eyes. His hands were wondrous, lifting her breasts, tenderly circling the nipples that peaked against his palms.

In a deep, raspy whisper, he said, "Open your eyes, Meggy. Look at us."

Like a puppet he could control with the touch of his fingers, she obeyed. The light was bright enough to highlight curves and lines, causing deep shadows. Their reflection in the mirror was erotic, wanton—her breasts filling his hands, his eyes burning like coals as he watched himself touch her.

One hand dipped lower and settled on her stomach as he stepped to her side. Heavy, pulsing, his sex nudged the curve of her hip. His fingers spread wide, cupping the rounded flesh that covered their child.

"You are beautiful," he said, wonder in his voice. "More beautiful than you've ever been."

Though her voice shook, she managed to quip, "You got a thing for pregnant ladies, Lieutenant?"

"Yeah." He grinned. "But mostly I've got a thing for this pregnant lady." Leaning forward, he pressed a kiss to the tip of her shoulder. The scrape of his beard, the moist movement of his tongue against her skin sent shivers through her body.

Her heart was beating so hard she thought he could hear it, but the only real sound in the room was the harsh intake of his breath. Or was it her breathing that filled the very air around them? She didn't know. She didn't care. Trembling, aching with need, she watched, hypnotized as Andy's hand edged ever lower across her belly, across the delta of dark curls, finally dipping in the dewy, waiting cleft. A groan of pleasure broke from her as their gazes met again in the mirror. He stroked, she opened to him, like a flower seeking the sun.

"I want you," she said, the words coming from a place deep inside her. "I want you more right now than I've ever wanted you." She turned into his arms, offering her mouth for his searching kiss.

She's like holding a dream, Andy thought as Meg's lips parted beneath his. She tasted of sweetness, her skin felt like silk. Breaking away, he trailed his mouth down the smooth, pure line of her neck. His tongue skimmed her flesh till he dipped his head and, with his lips, captured the tempting, pebbled tip of one breast. Gently he suckled, while Meg breathed his name, her hands pushing through his hair. He knelt then, pressing a kiss to her stomach, to the child that grew deep in her womb.

Turning his head, he looked in the mirror. They looked so right, so incredibly, completely right together. If only the rest of their lives could meld as their bodies did. If only he could always please Meg as he did now. He shut his eyes. Groaning at the intrusion of reality into this dreamlike moment, he stood, his hands cupping Meg's derriere as he lifted her up.

She protested, "Andy, don't . . . you can't carry—"

"Hush," he muttered, turning toward the bed. "Let me live out my fantasies. Just for tonight, okay? I feel very *adventurous.*"

Soft laughter greeted their old secret code word. "Show me," she whispered. "Show me how adventurous you can be."

Then he kissed her again. A deep kiss. Propelled by every night he had lain awake thinking of her. Strengthened by every regret he'd known over losing her. They kissed until their bodies pressed into the soft covers and giving pillows of the bed, till Meg's legs parted, till he drove himself deep into her.

And a thought that hadn't occurred to him all afternoon hit with full force. "This is okay, isn't it?" he asked. "For the baby, I mean?"

Her legs slipped high around his waist, and her words were punctuated by tiny gasps of pleasure as he moved inside her. "This . . . is . . . perfect."

Perfection wasn't nearly descriptive enough for the shattering explosion that followed. Andy felt as if he had fallen out of a plane without a chute. He floated nevertheless, wrapped tightly in Meg's embrace. His only wish before drifting off to sleep was that she never stop holding him.

It was nearly eleven before they awakened again that night. Meg was ravenous.

"I want the most incredibly, sinfully fattening food we can find in my kitchen," she told Andy as she slipped on her robe.

"Is that good for the baby?"

She patted her stomach. "This baby is going to enjoy whatever I feed it tonight."

So they grilled some sandwiches, spread liberally with butter and thick with cheese and ham. On the side were microwaved French fries, several packages, crisp and curly, ready to douse with catsup. For dessert, her refrigerator yielded vanilla ice cream, which Andy laced with chocolate syrup and topped with whipped cream.

In comfortable, companionable silence, they ate the sundaes in bed while watching a cable television news program. Nothing that had happened in the world during the day seemed as earthshaking to Meg as what had occurred between her and Andy.

But contrary to her usual pragmatic nature, she didn't want to discuss what had happened. If they started tearing it apart, she was sure they would argue. And it would be ruined. And for tonight, if only tonight, she wanted to savor the pleasure of going to sleep with Andy at her side. She had known other nights like this with him, when sanity was tossed aside. But this felt different. It felt important. She had a feeling that when she woke up in the morning, she wouldn't want to flee, as had been the case in the past. That confused her, but she didn't dwell on it. She just went to sleep in Andy's arms.

In the morning there was no fuss and bother over waking together. Andy kissed her, took a shower and hurried off to his place to dress. With the things she had left undone yesterday at the office, Meg had to get to work herself. But Andy called her midafternoon.

From the sounds in the background, she knew he was at a phone booth. He called to ask her to dinner that night, to tell her he had been thinking about her, about last night, all day.

Cradling the phone as he whispered sweet, naughty nothings, Meg giggled. Her secretary, who had been at Meg's desk when the phone rang, looked startled. Giggling wasn't something Meg did around the office on a regular basis. It didn't fit her image. But rather than getting off the phone as she might have done in times past, she swiveled her chair around to face the window and listened to Andy's highly erotic suggestions.

"You know," she murmured. "People are arrested for using phone lines for this purpose."

He chuckled. "I'm not worried. I have connections with the police department."

"You sound very corrupt."

"Corrupt. Decadent." His voice dropped to a deep seductive level. "Hot for you."

She giggled again, uncaring whether her secretary heard her or not. "This is sounding more and more promising."

"Are you sure I can't see you until tonight?"

She didn't bother worrying about the changes that were taking place in their relationship. She just wanted to see him. "Why don't I come straight to your place after work?"

He agreed and said goodbye, but instead of replacing the receiver immediately, Meg held it for a while as she stared out the window and thought about Andy.

Sighing, she finally turned... and caught her secretary standing in the doorway, staring.

Trying to stop the smile that was spreading across her face, Meg said, "Do you need me for something, Pamela?"

Though the younger woman flushed, she shook her head and tried in vain to hide her grin. Meg had to smile back. It was a rare, lighthearted moment between the two women. Though Meg always tried to treat her co-workers and employees with courtesy and respect, she didn't get too personally involved with any of them. She preferred to keep work and friendship as separate as possible. She knew very well that her pregnancy was the subject of office gossip. Her secretary had probably been hit with all the inquiries no one had dared ask directly. Now, with Meg giggling on the phone and smiling at nothing in particular, poor Pamela at last had something to talk about.

Still smiling, Meg returned to the series of calculations on her computer monitor, but her concentration was shot. So she moved on to other work on her desk. It was just as well. She had cut down on her time spent at the computer because of the studies she had read about the possible harmful effects of radiation during pregnancy. She was running behind on several projects, however, and what she needed to do was spend a couple of evenings playing catch-up.

Several months ago, Meg would have been ahead of her work schedule, not behind. Taking half the day off, as she had done yesterday, would have been out of the question. And she wouldn't now be thinking of taking off early again—just to see Andy.

She knew her superiors were watching her, wondering what effect the coming child would have on one of the company's most ambitious and productive employees. Meg was determined to carry on as she always had, but she didn't know what the baby would do to her hopes for a vice presidency. There were other candidates within the firm who had her qualifications and seniority. If she was passed over, it might be a blessing. A bigger job meant bigger responsibilities and more hours. As a single mother...

But you're not really alone, she reminded herself. There was Andy. Only he had a demanding job, too—erratic hours, lots of stress. Thinking of the schedules the two of them had tried to keep during their marriage, she heaved a gloomy sigh. None of this was going to be easy. She had seen many women burn out when they tried to have the fabled "all" of career and motherhood. And those women had been married, with their children's fathers firmly entrenched in the home with the child. How would it work with Andy? Would the baby have a room at his place, as well as hers? There were so many choices, decisions to be made.

The baby stirred inside her, and Meg brought her whirling thoughts under control. She forced herself to relax, closed her eyes and savored the fluttering movement in her womb. She was amazed, as always, by the life she was carrying. This baby had changed everything—affected the career she had once held so dear, drawn her back to Andy.

Would they be together without the baby? Would last night have happened if they hadn't become so emotional about the sonogram? She knew the answer was no. And that troubled her somewhat. Without even a pause, however, she had agreed to meet Andy again tonight. Here they were, practically playing house, exactly as she had vowed they wouldn't. But it was better than the cold distance that had been between them recently.

So what should she do?

Meg quickly realized the answer—she was going to go with the flow. And the flow led straight into Andy's arms. All her life she had planned and compartmentalized and projected. That had never worked with Andy. So maybe it was time to drift, to see where they might end up. Oh, she didn't expect miracles. Because of the baby there was a new dimension to their relationship, but for as long as she could remember, she had heard and read that a child couldn't repair what was broken. That was at least part of the argument she had used when she turned down Andy's marriage proposal. Without the baby, they still had only what they'd always had—great sex, a lot of laughs.

Thinking of last night's incredible loving sent a sudden burst of yearning through her. Why couldn't they put it all together? *If they tried. If they really tried once more . . .*

She laughed, called herself a fool and then let herself wish for the moon. Too many times during their marriage and in the years since, she had wondered if she and Andy couldn't try again. She didn't want to *try* this time. She didn't want to work at it, to hope too much. Instead, she knew she should concentrate on the little pieces that she and Andy always managed to get right. She should concentrate on tonight. Tomorrow she would worry about when it came.

Perhaps Andy sensed her come-what-may mood. For he didn't question their continued closeness over the next few weeks. And for the first time ever, she was content just to be with him. She didn't worry about what was missing or imperfect. In fact, the interlude was darn near perfect. They spent every free moment together. Dreaming aloud about the baby, walking in the fallen leaves with Boomer, carving a Halloween jack-o'-lantern, lying in bed while a cold November rain beat against the windows. Their lovemaking was intense, satisfying, as it had always been.

One hour, one minute, one day at a time. They took everything slow.

And there was a new ease between them. Before, Meg hadn't thought Andy listened when she tried to discuss her job with him. Now they talked, *really* talked about her ambitions, about the way the baby had altered her career plans. They covered almost all the old taboo subjects. Even visiting his parents and hers wasn't a major hassle. He still didn't talk much about his job, but Meg also didn't obsess about it the

way she used to. Oh, she was still frightened for him.
Nights when he had to be late, she worried. That might
never end. But there was an openness between them,
a maturity that often took her by surprise.

The Sunday before Thanksgiving, a big day in the
season's pro football race, Andy made a giant-sized
pot of chili at her place. Meg contributed corn bread,
baked in her Grandma Kathy's old, blackened cast-
iron skillet, the only way her family approved of corn
bread being made. Lisa and Terry, Will, Perri and Rod
and their brood came over to watch the game.

It was a mob scene. The dog barking, baby Jocelyn
crying, while those most interested in the game made
more noise cheering and booing than anyone under
seven. Especially since Lisa and Will were rooting for
opposing teams. The three little boys present did
plenty of running in and out of doors and clambering
up and down the stairs. Before she chased them into
safer regions of the house, Meg began to wish she had
chosen something other than silvery gray for her living room carpet, something more durable than a
lemon-yellow brocade for the couch.

During halftime, she supervised the boys' meal in
the kitchen's bay-windowed breakfast nook. The others gladly relinquished the children to her care and ate
in front of the sun room television. Jocelyn was asleep
in the now off-limits living room. And Boomer, who
had learned on previous visits which rooms he could
occupy, was catching a few winks of his own beside
Terry's chair. The arrangement pleased Meg. At least
in the kitchen, she knew any chili-painted handprints

she didn't intercept could be washed off the Mexican-tiled floor or painted over on the walls. By the end of the meal, she had made a mental vow not to take her own child to anyone's house until the age of twelve.

Finally she stood at the end of the table, doling out scoops of ice cream to the three rambunctious boys. "Now are you sure chocolate-chip mint ice cream is going to mix well with all that chili?"

"Sure, Mom." Andy slipped his arms around her from behind and nuzzled her neck. The kids exchanged sly glances and snickered. "She's gonna make a great mom, isn't she, guys?"

From the doorway behind them, Lisa answered, "She'll be a great mom, but her decor will definitely not make it. I found this upstairs when I went up to the bathroom." She held up a muddy football and fixed Terry with a challenging gaze. "This was in the bedroom that's going to be the baby's. Anybody know how it got there?"

Three "Not me's" rang out.

Lisa laughed. "Meg, Andy, in not so many years you will become very well acquainted with every child's best friend, whose name is 'Not Me.' He—or she—is an extremely bad influence." She opened the door leading to the deck and tossed the football outside. "Meg, you may want to reconsider the pale yellow carpet for the nursery."

Meg grinned at Andy. "Oh, I'm planning to redo it in shades of pink."

Before Andy could make his usual retort about the expected sex of their baby, Terry piped up, "Why isn't the baby going to live with you, Andy?"

An uneasy silence fell among the adults. Meg pulled out of Andy's arms and busied herself handing bowls of ice cream around the table.

Terry, apparently unaware of any undercurrents, reached down and patted the Irish setter's head. "I think Boomer might like having the baby over there."

Lisa grinned at Andy and said, "Why don't you take this one, Hotshot."

He tried to keep it light. "Well, Terry, my man." He ruffled the boy's straight blond hair. "You know Meg and I aren't married, don't you?"

"But can't you and Boomer move in here after the baby's born?"

Andy and Meg exchanged a glance before she started gathering up the bowls used for chili. He turned back to the earnest little boy. "No, Terry, Boomer and I will still live at my house. The baby is going to live here—with Meg, but he'll come over and see me a lot, too."

"Oh." Solemnly Terry scooped a spoonful of ice cream into his mouth. But there was still a troubled line between his eyebrows. "I was supposed to get to visit my dad, too." Wide and unblinking, his blue eyes looked up at Andy. "But I don't."

Andy exchanged a pleading glance with Lisa, who intervened, "It'll be different with Andy and Meg's baby, son."

"But why?"

"Because it will," she said with a mother's firmness. "Now stop asking questions and eat your ice cream."

From the sun room, Rod called, "Halftime's over."

The boys, who hadn't cared about the game before, now ran whooping into the other room, abandoning the dessert they had demanded. Boomer chased after them, barking. And again, the three adults stood in awkward silence.

Andy watched Meg finish stacking chili bowls. In a falsely bright voice, she said, "Look at this, the guys did great. Not even a chili bean on the floor. And here I thought I'd be scraping dried meat off the ceiling for days."

Lisa took the bowls out of her hands. "Why don't you go in there and sit down for a while? You've been racing around after those kids all day. Me and Hotshot'll clean up this mess."

"But the game—"

"Is pretty darn boring, anyway. Espinoza's team is winning." She steered Meg toward the door and gave her a little push.

When she was gone, Andy shook his head and muttered out the side of his mouth, "I recognize the look, Lisa. You're about to give me one of your famous lectures. I can do without it." Juggling all three still-full bowls of ice cream, he headed for the refrigerator.

Lisa directed a glance over her shoulder toward the sun room, as if she expected Meg to reappear at any moment. She set her load of bowls in the sink. "What are you two doing?'' she demanded in a stage whisper.

Ignoring her, Andy placed the ice cream in the freezer. ''You think the boys will eat this later?''

''Just answer the question.'' Lisa switched on the faucet and began rinsing the dishes, using the running water as a cover to say, ''A month ago, you two were having a baby, but the relationship was kaput. Now you're together all the time. Do you realize the only times I've seen you recently have been down at the precinct?''

''I've been busy.''

''Obviously. Now you and Meg are sharing these little looks—''

''What looks?''

''And you're kissing her on the neck.''

''Is that a crime?''

''It is if this is another one of your famous hit-and-run hot streaks.''

Andy blinked. ''You want to run that last part by me one more time?''

''Hit-and-run hot streaks,'' Lisa repeated as she dumped silverware into its compartment in the dishwasher. ''You know exactly what they are—you made that baby during one of them. I hope this is more than that—for the baby's sake.''

Realizing the open freezer door was pouring cold air into his face, Andy slammed it shut and stalked back to the table to gather up dirty glasses and crumpled paper napkins. He wasn't angry with Lisa. It was that she had reminded him of how he and Meg were merely drifting through the days. Not that he didn't enjoy the drifting, but occasionally he wondered what they were doing, where they were heading.

Months before, when he had tried to distance himself from Meg, he had been trying to protect his heart. Then he had turned around and placed it in jeopardy once more. Only this time, his broken heart would hurt much, much more. Because the past few weeks with Meg had been like having a good, long vacation in heaven. But that was all they had been—an interlude, a pause. Oh, they were getting along great. But where was it leading them? Were they truly making some progress on a future together? He didn't think so.

"I don't want to see you hurt," Lisa said quietly.

Nodding, he placed the glasses in the dishwasher. "It's under control," he lied. "We've got it figured out."

He could feel Lisa's disbelieving glance, but he walked away, unwilling to share his fears with even his closest friend.

In the sun room, he dragged a big overstuffed floor pillow next to Meg, who had curled into her favorite, brightly cushioned chair with a magazine. The boys had rambled out onto the back deck once more, Lisa was still in the kitchen, and Perri, Rod and Will were caught up in the game. Andy tried to summon some enthusiasm for the contest, but Lisa's words kept chasing around and around in his head.

What are you two doing?

Meg had once called it playing house. Perhaps she was right. And maybe he wanted to stop. Because he loved her, had always loved her, always would. That confession was no real revelation. The love had always been there. But it would take more than love to solidify what they had together. Hell, he had always known that. If only he knew how to do it, how to make Meg truly happy.

She interrupted his agonizing with a touch on his shoulder. She handed the magazine down to him, tapping the left side of a page. "Wouldn't this be great in the nursery?"

The room pictured in the layout was bright and sunshine filled. Carousel horses, festooned with ribbons and flowers, were painted on one wall, while a striped awning, much like a circus tent, draped the ceiling. Andy thought any child, boy or girl, would probably love this room. Bleakly he wondered if they could do two versions—one for here, another for his house.

Perhaps his gloomy thoughts were reflected in his face, because when he glanced up at Meg, her smile dimmed and disappeared. "Andy?"

He forced a laugh and took the magazine from her hand. "Sure, we can do this. Are you going to paint the carousel horses? Mine would be stick figures."

Meg laughed, too, but she sat back in the chair, wondering about the agonized look she had seen on Andy's face. Surely he wasn't really upset by the remark Terry had made earlier. It was awkward, trying to explain their situation to a child, to anyone, for that matter, but that shouldn't have caused the look of pure pain she had witnessed.

But of course Andy wouldn't talk about it.

Later, after everyone had gone home, she asked him if something was wrong. He shook his head in that stubborn, implacable way she remembered all too well and said nothing. And as she had in the past, she became irritated. "It's obvious that something's bothering you, Andy. Why can't we talk about it?"

He wanted to talk. Hell, he longed to tell her he loved her, to ask her what she thought about the past few weeks, about their future together. But there was a risk involved in showing all his feelings. She could throw them back in his face, tell him they had no future. She could make everything worse than it already was. No, it was easier to try to sort all this out alone.

So they had a scene not unlike one of their arguments during their marriage—with Meg demanding and him resisting. And for the first time in a month, they spent the night apart.

On the phone the next day, he offered an awkward apology. Her acceptance was just as stiff. They didn't see or talk to each other on Tuesday. Wednesday evening, early, Meg started calling his place. There was no answer, and she quickly became annoyed.

They had made tentative plans to go to his parents' house for Thanksgiving dinner, but she didn't know an exact time. She called his mother but didn't tell her she hadn't talked to Andy. Meg assured Lucy they would be over at one the next day. Then she brewed a cup of herb tea and went to bed with some work she had brought home from the office. At ten, when there was still no word from Andy, she began to get really angry. Where was he?

A cold wind rattled the few remaining leaves on the tree outside her bedroom window. She burrowed deeper in the covers, imagining all sorts of terrible things that could have happened to Andy. Too vividly she recalled similar nights when she had waited for him to come home and the arguments that had ensued when she confronted him with her anger and worry. She didn't like those memories. She told herself she wasn't going to repeat those mistakes.

But while she was dialing his number for what seemed like the hundredth time that night, the doorbell chimed and she heard the front door open downstairs. Andy's voice traveled up the stairs, "Meg?"

In that moment she regretted ever giving him a key to her place. She would have dearly loved to make him wait outside in the cold for a while. But she wasn't giving in to anger. Scrambling for a book from the bedside table, she settled against her pillows, adopted an air of unconcern and called for him to come upstairs. Her faked nonchalance fled when he appeared in the doorway.

Andy looked terrible. His cheeks were ruddy, as if he had stood too long in the driving November wind. Beneath the windburn, he was pale, his eyes bloodshot. His shoulders drooped as he crossed the room.

Anger forgotten, Meg set her book aside. "What's wrong?"

He shook his head, shrugged out of his jacket and kicked off his shoes before climbing, still dressed, into bed next to her.

Something was wrong. That much was plain to see. But his obvious distress was a surprise. Hiding his feelings was more Andy's style. She turned on her side. Experience told her to go easy. Tentatively she touched his hair. "Andy? Do you need anything?"

He shook his head and closed his eyes. "Bad day," he mumbled.

She replied with the three words she had vowed not to use, "I was worried."

He didn't react with anger. Instead, he turned over and drew her body tight to his. "I'm sorry I didn't call yesterday. Or today."

In the warmth of the covers, cold still clung to him—to the crisp cotton of his khaki slacks, to his wrinkled blue shirt, to his hands. He felt stiff with the cold. "You're freezing," Meg murmured, hugging him close.

"It's a damn cold night."

She pulled away, ready to stroke a comforting hand through his hair again, yet the expression on his face stopped her. His eyes were clenched shut, but a tear, a tiny but unmistakable tear had escaped and was running down one cheek. She was astounded. Andy never cried. He might see horror, might hurt, but he didn't react. *What had happened?* Gently, with trembling fingers, she brushed the telltale drop of moisture away.

And he looked up at her, lashes damp around those blue, blue eyes of his. "There was this kid, Meg...." He swallowed, closed his eyes again.

She waited, not moving, not daring to say anything.

He took a deep breath. "He was dead when we got there, Meg...dead...and it just reminded me..." His voice was rough with emotion, but the last few words came out clearly anyway. "He reminded me of David. The way it happened was so like David...."

And then Meg cried. Because Andy still wouldn't, couldn't let go enough to really cry, she cried for him.

Chapter Eight

Andy lay, holding Meg close, and he felt some of the day's horror begin to ebb. God, it felt good to be here. The warmth of Meg's body was finally chasing the chill out of his bones. Ever since he and Will had arrived at the convenience store where that young, innocent kid lay dead, he had wanted to run here, to be safe and secure, away from his old nightmares.

But the nightmares hadn't been outrun. They were here, too, trembling on his lips, waiting to be told.

In his eleven years on the force, he had seen plenty of senseless deaths, acts of violence and rage. The odds had always been good that one day he would run into a situation similar to the one that had confronted him and his brother years ago. Tonight had been the night.

"Tell me," Meg whispered as she wiped the tears from her cheeks. "What happened, Andy? Who was it that reminded you of David?"

Years ago, Andy would have shut his eyes and blocked her questions out. He would have said she didn't understand. He would have hidden his anguish. His reasoning had been that if she heard how bad it had been or saw how upset he was, her fears for him would grow. And there were his own anxieties to contend with, as well—the feelings of hopelessness and despair that followed a night like tonight. To Andy, if you shared those feelings with someone, you had to confront them yourself. He preferred to lock them away, to pretend they didn't exist.

The counselor he had seen years ago had talked about what happened when feelings were hidden, how they could build up inside you and explode. But Andy had always figured you were pretty weak if you couldn't control your own thoughts and fears. And to him, weakness was intolerable.

Tonight, however, was different. Perhaps tonight, the explosion point he had scoffed at had been reached. Tonight, he had run to Meg. And he hadn't bothered to hide the ache inside him.

She repeated his name softly, letting him know she was still waiting for an explanation.

He drew away and sat up. "I am really sorry I didn't call you."

She pushed herself up, too. "It isn't that you owe me a phone call or anything—"

"Yes, I do owe you. I..." He closed his eyes. All his uncertainties about their relationship came rushing back. In his haste to get here, he had forgotten about the strain that had been between them these last few days.

Meg slipped her hand through the crook of his elbow. "I couldn't help but wonder where you were. With Thanksgiving tomorrow—"

He gave a short laugh and leaned against the headboard. "Thanksgiving. Man, what a great way to start a holiday."

"Please tell me what happened. I want to know."

He couldn't sit still, not while today's events kept replaying again and again in his head. So he got up and began to pace as he explained, "Will and I were coming in after having been out on a case most of the afternoon. We had paperwork to do, and it was getting late. We both wanted to go home. But first there was a call...an apparent murder not two blocks from where we were."

"Wouldn't a patrol car be sent first?"

"Officers were already on the scene. We were dispatched as the homicide team." He closed his eyes, remembering the mayhem that had greeted them when he and Will arrived.

The convenience store's harsh neon lights were vivid against the low, gray clouds of the fading November afternoon. A crowd, held at bay by officers, had already gathered in the parking lot. Women shrieked their sorrow. Children cried. Men mumbled in deep, angry voices. From the covered figure on the concrete in front of the store came no sound at all.

Andy stopped pacing, still seeing the slight, unmoving form, though it was Meg he looked at. "The kid who died was fifteen. A neighborhood boy. The store has a couple of video games, and he and his buddies liked to hang out and play them sometimes. The afternoon clerk said they were good kids, really good...." Remembering the clerk's devastation, he shook his head. "The kid came in today alone, to buy some brown sugar for his mother's Thanksgiving Day pecan pie."

"Who killed him?"

"I wish I knew."

"There was no description?"

"Sure, but it could fit a thousand people—a couple of toughs in a nondescript car, out to knock over a few convenience stores for some money to see 'em through the holiday weekend." Andy swallowed hard. "Instead of laying low in the back of the store, the kid tried to sneak out the door in the middle of the holdup. He started screaming for help once he got outside. One of the punks panicked and shot him."

Meg's dark eyes were wide with horror. "They'll be caught, won't they?"

Andy turned away, shrugging.

"You'll catch them," she assured him. "The famous Andy Baskin instincts, remember?"

Hands closing into fists at his side, he drew in a deep shuddering breath and released it as he fought the memories that were pulling at him. "So what if I do catch them?"

"Justice will be served."

"It won't bring that kid back." He looked at Meg. "They caught the bum who killed David. And justice didn't help me much."

She slipped out of bed and came to him, pressing her face to his chest as her arms slipped around his waist. "Oh, Andy, I know you still grieve for him. I wish you could have some peace about it."

"David was fifteen, too, you know," Andy murmured as he rested his cheek against Meg's soft hair. "Like that kid today. David's sixteenth birthday was only two weeks away when he died."

She hugged him tighter. "Tell me about David. What was he like?"

"You've seen his picture."

"He didn't look much like you."

Andy sighed. "We were really different in other ways, too. I was the clown in school, always called on the carpet for cutting up or raising hell. David was smarter, quieter, better behaved. But he wasn't a nerd. He was just sort of... intense."

She drew away, looking up at him. "Like your Dad?"

"Oh, no, not like Dad," Andy said quickly. "I could talk to David. Tell him things." Then he frowned. For the first time he wondered if perhaps David was like their father might have been, before life's disappointments turned him into a sour old man.

"Sounds as if you and David were close."

"Oh, we had our battles. He was almost four years older, so of course he was always trying to tell me what to do." He grinned at a sudden memory. "David explained sex to me, except there were parts that he had all wrong, and I went around for years thinking..." He paused, his face growing red. "Well, never mind what I thought."

Meg laughed softly. "Tell me."

"Some things are better left between brothers." With those words, Andy's smile died. *Between brothers*. In the end, it had been between them. A choice. One of them lived, one died.

"What is it?" Meg asked him. "What are you thinking?"

Andy didn't consider not answering. Though his throat was tight, choked by the force of his memories, he said, "I was remembering the day he died. It was one of those long, long summer afternoons. Remember how long they used to be?"

Nodding, she took his hands in hers, threading their fingers together. Her gaze was steady on his. "Hours were like days back then."

"It was so hot that summer." Remembering, Andy could almost feel the July humidity pressing down on him. That day the sun was fierce enough to turn the tar on the road to a soft black pitch. Even air conditioners were hard-pressed to cut the stifling Georgia air.

"We had been mowing grass all day," he continued, focusing on a point above Meg's shoulder. "David was still too young to get a job that summer, so he and I mowed some neighbors' lawns for extra cash.

That day, Mom told us to come inside, to cool off. We were thirsty, but we had drunk all the soft drinks in the house, and she said she wasn't going to the market for more right then." He stopped, remembering that his mother had been pressing his father's white shirts that day. His father liked his shirts a certain way, something no dry cleaners had ever managed to get right. Andy could still smell the spray starch, hear the sizzle of the iron as his mother pushed it across the white cotton.

"She offered us water, lemonade, iced teas," he murmured. "But that wouldn't do, of course. She was hot and irritable, too, and she got mad at us. We said we were going to walk down to this little neighborhood store that was up on the main road, and she said no—you know, the way mothers say no just because you've asked too often."

"I guess all mothers are the same."

"So are all boys." He drew in a ragged breath. "So we snuck out when she got busy in another part of the house. I remember later..." He broke off, felt the tears fill his eyes. "Later, she kept saying, 'if only I had gone to the store.'"

Meg gripped his hands tighter. "I'm sure she's tortured herself about that."

Fighting the pain that rose through him, he nodded. "I guess we all have some 'if onlys' about that day. If only I hadn't been with David, if only he hadn't pushed me—"

"Don't," Meg said. "Don't focus on what might have been different. It only deepens the hurt."

But he closed his eyes, anyway, as he had done a thousand times, and he wished for a different end to that sweltering summer afternoon. Unfortunately, however, nothing ever changed about these memories. By sharing them with Meg, they became sharper still.

As he remembered it, the walk to the store was long and hot, so hot he and David weren't expending any energy on conversation by the time they got there. The store was empty save for the clerk at the front. They bought a couple of cold drinks and gulped them down right away, selected a few more and, without even arguing, went down another aisle to get a bag of chips. They were at the back of the store when the bells on the front door jangled, signaling another customer. Andy remembered some loud conversation as he started up the aisle.

Then the clerk called out a warning.

And the customer whipped around. A tall man, his face red, eyes glittering. A gun in his hand.

Andy heard a click just as his brother shoved him down from behind.

He never heard the gunshot.

He remembered only the cans that fell as David's body slammed into the shelves. He turned just in time to see the red spot that bloomed on the front of David's grass-stained T-shirt. And David's face. He would never forget David's expression—the startled look in his blue eyes. It lasted only half a second, then David pitched forward, his body covering Andy, flattening him onto the floor. Everything else was black.

He could feel that blackness swallowing him, even now.

"Andy?" Meg's touch was cool on his face, cool as the tiled floor of that store had been. Her touch brought him reeling back to the present. Only then did he realize he had tears on his cheeks to match her own.

He jerked away. "Dammit, Meg, I'm sorry—"

"Don't," she whispered, her fingers closing on his upper arms as she forced him to look at her. "Don't say you're sorry for feeling, Andy. He was your brother, and he was killed, and it was horrible, and you have a right to still feel that pain."

He shook his head. "It happened over twenty years ago. It shouldn't feel so immediate. I shouldn't have lost it when I saw that kid tonight."

She looked as if she didn't believe him. "And how did you lose it?"

"I couldn't function. I couldn't look at the boy without seeing David. I couldn't even think." He ran a hand over his face. "Dammit, Meg, I got so upset I was sick. Will was in there doing the job, and I was in the restroom, throwing up."

There were traces of tears on her face, but with chin tilted upward, she challenged him, "So what if you lost it this once?"

"So that's not how I operate."

"Oh, no," she murmured. "No, you're always so cool. You laugh things off. You don't *feel* anything. When David died, you just closed down inside, didn't you? I bet you never even cried for him."

"Of course I did."

"When? In your room, where no one could see you?"

"I was a boy. Boys aren't supposed to sit around crying."

"Who says?"

"Everyone."

"Including your parents, I guess."

"Maybe..." He shook his head. "I don't remember."

"Did they cry with you?"

He looked away, not willing to admit the truth. During the rest of that endless, heat-soaked summer, his parents' home had become the divided, quiet place it was now. His father, never a demonstrative man, had pulled completely inside himself. His mother had tried to reach out to him, but she was struggling with the pain herself. "You have to understand," he said to Meg. "The grief was so unbearable, so complete. Things like this weren't supposed to happen to us."

"I agree. Things this horrible should never happen to twelve-year-old boys."

"Not to anyone."

"But especially not to a little boy," she insisted. "What did your parents do to try and help you? I mean, you saw your brother die. Didn't they talk about it with you?"

He frowned, trying to remember. "Mom did. She said I wasn't ever to think it was my fault."

"Did you believe her?"

Andy didn't answer. Again, he relived those moments when David shoved him aside, when the bullet hit David's chest and knocked him back against the shelves. As an adult, he could see none of it was his fault. But as a child, as a scared, frightened child, he had wondered and worried and prayed to God to forgive him.

Looking up, he saw Meg still waiting for an answer. He cleared his throat. "It was hard to believe I wasn't to blame," he admitted. "Everybody kept saying how brave David had been, how he had saved me." He looked up at the ceiling. "And I just wanted to die."

"Your parents—"

"Did the best they could," Andy cut in, an edge of irritation in his voice. "Maybe they didn't fall all over themselves reassuring me, but you can't know what it was like for them. They just tried to carry on as normal."

She looked unconvinced. "I guess that's why there are no pictures of David around. That way they could pretend he didn't exist."

"That's not true," he protested. "Mom and I remembered him. She'd come in my room every night, like she'd done when I was really small, and we'd talk about David. Together, we tried to keep him alive—for a while, anyway. Then . . . I guess she couldn't anymore. Maybe it hurt too much."

"But your father didn't talk about him?"

"I tried to get him to a few times, but he couldn't. Even at the funeral . . ." Andy stopped. David's funeral was one memory too many. "Everyone said Dad took it all pretty well."

Meg's hands clenched over her stomach. "He took it well? My God, Andy, he lost a son. He almost lost you, too. Why should anyone take that well?"

"He couldn't just fall apart," Andy retorted. "He had to be strong. For me. For Mom."

"How strong is it to shut a little boy out?"

Andy tried not to think of the times when he had ached for a kind word from his father, when he had waited to be noticed. Despite those times, he had grown up thinking of his father as a strong, in-control person, everything a man should be. He had resented his coldness, yes, but he had never questioned his father's strength. All his life, Andy had wanted to be as tough as his father and as brave as the brother who had died for him.

Accordingly he defended his father to Meg, "Dad and I were never really close, not even before David was killed."

"I guess that meant you didn't need him."

"Of course I needed him."

"But he was never there for you. Your mother told me that."

Andy turned from her and sank down onto the edge of the bed, his shoulders slumping. "Meg, I don't want to argue about what my father did or didn't do. He is what he is. And I'm what I..." His mouth closed as he considered the conclusions he was drawing.

"Like father like son?" she murmured.

"No," Andy said quickly. "I'm not like him." He thought back to the day Meg had told him about the baby. He had vowed then to be a different kind of father, to try to be a different kind of man. "I'd never treat our child the way my father treated me."

"So you're promising you won't shut her out the way you shut me out?"

Andy looked up at Meg. Tears were glittering in her eyes again. God, how he hated to see her cry. "I never intended—"

"Yes, you do," Meg shot back at him. "You intentionally slam doors in my face. That's what ended it for us years ago. Whenever I reached out, you dropped back. Even when you were hurting, you wouldn't let me in."

He hung his head, knowing what she said was true. "I wanted to spare you."

"But you didn't. Remember that night when you were shot?"

Andy's head snapped up. "We don't need to re-hash that, Meg. You know Lisa and I—"

"Now I know there was nothing between you," Meg interrupted. "But I didn't then. I got a call, telling me you'd been hurt. I rushed over to the hospital, expecting you to be dead. But there you were with Lisa..." She spun away from him, again feeling the pain she had known that night. She could still see Andy's head bent so close to the other woman's blond hair. She knew now that there had been nothing romantic in the moment. It was one officer comforting another who had been injured. But they had been connecting. In ways that Andy never connected with Meg.

She felt his hands on her shoulders. "We've been through this before. Why do it again?"

"Because that's the night our marriage ended."

His hands fell away. "You wouldn't listen to me, Meg."

She turned around, determined to confront him on this for the last time. "Because there was nothing left to say. I wasn't important to you. You didn't need me. You didn't want to share anything more than a bed with me."

His eyes narrowed. "That's not true. I wanted a life with you, a child, a home."

"And I wanted to wait. But you wouldn't listen to what I wanted. For you, there was no middle ground, no room for compromise. It was your way or no way, and when I wouldn't bow to your every wish, you cut me out."

Voice bitter, he said, "I didn't see how I fit in your plans."

In a tired gesture, she drew her hand through her hair. "It's because you wouldn't talk to me, Andy. You wouldn't listen. You wouldn't answer my questions. When I wanted to talk about your job, about the dangers, about how waiting for you to come home night after night made me feel, you told me I didn't understand, that I couldn't understand what being a cop meant to you."

"It is hard to explain."

"You've never tried. When we got married, you told me you were going to go to law school."

"That was a maybe—"

"Which you never intended to follow through."

His mouth set in a thin line. "I'm a cop, Meg. Being a cop is the only way..." He stopped, the muscles in his throat working.

But Meg wouldn't let him retreat. "The only way what? To make up for David?"

His words came out in a rush. "That's how it began, yeah, I wanted to be a hero, like my big brother. Somebody my parents might be proud of."

Meg bit her lip, remembering all of his accomplishments that she had heard about from Will and Lisa. Andy was a hero, though she doubted his parents knew. She hadn't bothered to find out herself. "What about now?" she whispered. "Why are you still a cop?"

He shrugged, and she could see him trying to formulate a brash, cocky answer. But for once, he didn't. Instead, he looked her straight in the eye, and she would bet her life his answer came direct from his heart, "I guess I'm trying to make a difference. Maybe trying to keep one more kid alive."

Feeling as if they had broken through some invisible barrier, she stepped forward and put her arms around him. "You do make a difference. And I'm proud of you for that. I'm still frightened for you, but I'm proud."

He drew away, amazement in his expression. "You never said that before."

She managed a shaky laugh. "Because we've never talked like this before." Tenderly she touched his face.

"Do you realize how often we've talked all *around* these issues without really talking at all?"

"Too many times," he admitted.

They stood, looking at each other, a new understanding beginning to blossom between them. Seconds ticked by with only the sound of the wind whispering around the corner of the building.

Finally Andy said, "Come here," and he sat down on the edge of the bed, pulling Meg into his lap. Solemnly he said, "I've made a lot of mistakes."

"We both have."

"But when we were married, I was young and full of myself, trying to prove something to someone. Maybe just trying to be noticed. I don't want to make those mistakes now."

A fluttering, expectant feeling started somewhere near her heart. What was Andy trying to say?

He placed his hand on her stomach. "It's the baby. He's changed the way I look at everything. My job, who I am, who I want to be."

The baby. Meg knew a familiar stab of disappointment at his words. It always came back to the baby. Without the baby, she and Andy wouldn't be working any of this out. If it wasn't for the baby, would Andy have come running to her tonight? Would he have finally opened up and talked about David? She didn't know. She wondered if she'd ever be sure.

And that mattered. She had tried to tell herself it didn't matter why he was in her life. But it did. A great deal. She was tired of drifting, of not knowing what the future held. Meg wanted Andy to care about her.

Just her. If she was completely honest with herself, she had wanted that from the beginning. That's why she had felt so much jealousy when all he had talked about was their child.

Oh, she wanted him to love the baby. Choosing between her or their child wasn't the point, but she wanted to be sure of Andy's love for her. Weeks ago, she had thought she might be able to settle for the parts she and Andy could get right. But now she wanted all the pieces of this puzzle they called a relationship. The passion. The laughter. And finally—at long last—the love and the sharing of their lives.

She wanted to win Andy's heart again.

She knew tonight was a start, a new beginning. He had come to her, seeking comfort, ready to share some long-kept secrets. His doing so showed that Andy was different, that something good had happened between them. It was a new foundation on which to build. But she wasn't going to ask Andy for promises. Everything had always happened too fast between them. She always made too many demands. Waiting for this baby to be born was teaching her something about patience, something she should apply to herself and Andy. If she was patient, she might finally have it all.

So she snuggled close to him. "I'm glad you've changed. This baby is changing us both. For the better."

With a hand under her chin, he lifted her face, and his lips moved sweetly on hers. As always, there was the promise of heat in his kiss. Sighing, Meg moved closer, her fingers fumbling with the buttons of his shirt. She slipped her hand inside, stroking the light furring of hair on his chest, savoring the warmth of his skin.

"I missed you the last few nights," he breathed against her mouth.

"How much?"

"Let me show you."

With kisses and touches and whispers of promised passion, he urged her back on the bed. Her gown slipped up and off. His clothes followed suit. And his hands were on her. Everywhere. He touched her lightly. Insistently. With agonizing tenderness. Until her skin was flushed and damp. Until the heat inside her roiled. She slipped her body over his, moved with him, till they found trembling, complete release.

And in the heart-racing, returning-to-earth aftermath, Andy began to chuckle.

Meg gazed at him in astonishment. "If I weren't so gloriously sated, I might be hurt."

"Don't be." Turning on his side, Andy propped himself up on his elbow. With his other hand, he gently stroked her rounded stomach in a slow, circular motion. "I was just thinking that no matter what we do we always seem to wind up in bed."

She giggled, her hand settling over his. "The flesh is weak, Baskin."

"Even when the mind is made up." His smile faded. "I left here Sunday night once more determined that we wouldn't do this again."

She frowned. "I never did understand what happened on Sunday."

"Lisa made me see that you and I were playing games again."

"Lisa's pretty observant, isn't she?"

"Too observant sometimes." Andy drew the covers over them and settled next to Meg again, his blue-eyed gaze steady on hers. "I don't want to play anymore."

"Neither do I."

"What does that mean?"

"You tell me."

Lying face-to-face, they regarded each other for a moment that stretched into several. Then, with a sigh, Andy turned on his back. Just when Meg thought he wasn't going to say anything, his hand clasped hers. "I guess what we have to do is try again, Meg. I'm willing to try."

"So am I."

Those simple words were enough for Andy tonight. He had talked so much, shown all his weaknesses, displayed half his fears. So for right now, it was enough to cradle Meg's hand in his own.

Tomorrow there would be time to start building something together.

Chapter Nine

Andy couldn't remember a better Christmas season. Because he was happy, there was an extra bit of excitement in the air. The holiday lights were brighter. The traditional seasonal carols took on new meaning. He actually enjoyed shopping, mixing with the throngs of people in the malls. Though her advancing pregnancy had slowed Meg down, she was in her element, decorating her condo and his house, buying an excessive number of gifts for everyone she loved.

On Christmas Eve, Andy and Meg went to his parents' for an early dinner and to open their packages. Maybe it was Meg's infectious charm. Or perhaps it was simply the magic of the season. For whatever the reason, even Andy's father seemed mellower than

usual. As he carved the turkey, he said it was an aw-
fully big bird for only four people. Then he actually
smiled in Meg's direction. "Of course, one of us is
eating for two."

Andy's mother reprimanded him. "Oh, Karl, that's
such an old-fashioned idea. I'm sure Meg is watching
what she eats very carefully."

Meg grinned and passed her plate to Karl. "That's
right. I'll very carefully take several slices of turkey."

They all laughed. And after dinner, they opened
packages. Meg saved one of Karl's gifts for the last. It
was a T-shirt with "World-Class Granddad" embla-
zoned across the front in gold, glittery letters.

Andy watched his father stare at the front of the
shirt in astounded silence for several moments. Andy
waited, expecting some sort of reaction, but his father only thanked Meg and folded the shirt back into
the box.

Later, while Meg and Lucy were in the kitchen,
slicing the desserts they hadn't been able to eat right
after dinner, Karl cleared his throat and asked, "So,
son, what are you and Meg going to do?"

Surprised, Andy looked at him.

His father continued, "What I mean is, are you
going to marry her?"

"That's . . . uh . . . kind of up in the air right now."

"Oh." Karl crossed his arms and stared at the television set, where Jimmy Stewart was acting out an ordinary life in a classic holiday movie. For a minute,
Andy thought his father was caught up in the movie.

But then he added, "I've never told you what to do with your life, Andy."

"No, sir, you haven't." *You never told me much at all.*

"I won't start now." There was a pause. "However, I do think you and Meg should marry. It would be the best for the child."

"Maybe you're right."

His father nodded. Eyes narrowed, he watched the television screen again. Andy turned to watch it, too. The ordinary man in the movie had discovered he'd had a wonderful life. As Stewart ran through the snow, Andy's father smiled again. "This is your mother's favorite part. I bet she's seen it a hundred times. Not the whole movie. Just this part." He shook his head. "I've never seen what's so great about it."

Lucy came into the den at that point, bringing Karl a slice of coconut cake and fussing at him for not telling her the movie was on. She perched on the arm of Karl's chair and cried as the movie reached its sentimental climax. But it wasn't his mother's tears that surprised Andy. It was the way his father looked at her. With indulgence. And affection. And as the credits rolled and Lucy sighed, she leaned for a moment against her husband's shoulder.

Suddenly Andy realized his parents still loved each other. Despite all the pain over David's death, the coldness that had settled over his father, there was still love here. It wasn't a grand passion. But something of their love had survived all these years. The thought gave him a warm feeling.

And before he and Meg left, he went and stood in the room he had once shared with David. His mother had changed the decor and put away the souvenirs and trophies he had left behind, but the twin beds were in the same spots they had always stood.

Right after David died, Andy used to stare at the empty bed across from his. And sometimes, in the dark, he'd think he heard David whisper his name. Tonight he heard laughter. Funny, how he had forgotten the way they used to laugh in this room, in this house. Despite the damper his father had sometimes placed on things, they had found something to laugh about.

And maybe the laughter was what he should start remembering.

From the living room, his mother called, "Andy, where are you?" It was the same tone she had used when he was eight, ten, seventeen. There was something reassuring about that sameness.

Smiling, he turned to take Meg home.

Later that evening, he knelt next to the tree in her living room and sorted through a pile of gifts marked *For Our Baby*. He glanced at Meg, who was coming in from the kitchen with a tray of cookies and eggnog in her hands and Boomer at her heels. "Meg, the kid's not even here, and already you're spoiling him."

"Those are all things the baby will need." Meg laughed and used her elbow to flip off the overhead lights, so that the room was bathed only in the glow of the Christmas tree's multicolored bulbs. "I thought it was nicer to wrap them up and put them under the tree.''

"No wonder you're a vice president. You have an answer for everything."

"Vice president." Her laughter trilled out again. "Can you believe they actually took a chance and made this pregnant woman a vice president?"

"It wasn't really a chance. You were obviously right for the job—baby or no baby."

The promotion, offered in early December, had been a surprise. In mid-February, she would be taking a six-week maternity leave at the height of tax season, when they were busiest. So she hadn't expected any kind of offer, if it came at all, until well after the baby was born. And Andy knew Meg had agonized over her decision to accept the new position. But the firm's president had expressed confidence in her ability to juggle motherhood and the added responsibilities. He said they were going to be supportive of her. At the same time, Meg said she knew her performance would be scrutinized as closely as any other VP.

Andy worried about the pressures Meg was going to be under. Was already under, he corrected. She had been putting in some long hours. He had been honest with her about his worries. They had talked the situation through, but he hadn't discouraged her. He had promised to do all he could to help her make it work.

He took the tray she offered, set it aside and gave her a hand as she took a seat on the floor next to him. "What do the big guys say when you waddle into the executive meetings?"

"I don't waddle!"

He eyed her round pumpkin of a stomach and lifted an eyebrow.

"But I don't want to waddle," she cried, aghast. "God, Andy, there are almost two months left to go. How am I going to move?"

"We could check into renting a crane." He dodged the mock-serious blow she directed at him.

"You're rotten, Andy Baskin. Last night you were telling me how much you like me being plump."

"Last night I was in the throes of passion."

This time she punched him in the arm. "I always knew you lied to get me in bed. You're despicable." She turned, calling for the dog. "Get him, Boomer, get...Boomer!" Her command turned into a dismayed croak. For Boomer had stolen a Christmas cookie from the tray and was busily crumbling it all over the carpet.

Andy laughed at Meg's horrified expression. She had only recently allowed Boomer in any room in her condo other than the kitchen. The dog had been behaving himself, too. Up until now. "It's that tie you made him wear," Andy said.

As if he understood, Boomer whined and scratched at the silly green-and-red-plaid bow tie Meg had placed around his collar.

"We're establishing traditions," she said primly. "For the baby. From now on, we're going to dress up a little on Christmas Eve. That includes Boomer."

The dog whined again and rolled over in his cookie crumbs. Meg groaned, mumbling something about undisciplined mutts.

"It's his first time in a tie," Andy said in his dog's defense. "Cut him some slack."

"Well, at least you look nice." She smiled at him in approval. "You're very fashionable tonight, Lieutenant Baskin."

He slipped an arm around her shoulders and pressed a kiss to her temple. "If I'm fashionable, you're responsible." His charcoal-gray slacks and burgundy cardigan sweater were early Christmas gifts from her. Like a kid unable to wait for the holiday, she had been passing out presents for days. The funny thing was, the stack of gifts under the tree didn't seem to be diminishing much.

"Do I really waddle?" she asked in a small voice.

He grinned, kissed her again. "Of course not. You look beautiful."

That wasn't idle reassurance. Meg looked wonderful. She glowed with good health. No, her figure was no longer sleek, but the extra pounds added a becoming softness to her features. And he doubted anything could alter the air of sophistication that always clung to her. Tonight, she wore white slacks with a matching, oversize, fuzzy sweater dotted with sequins and beads. They reflected the lights from the tree but were no brighter than her eyes, no glossier than her shining ebony hair. He loved the way she looked, plump with his child, serene, confident—a very modern madonna.

Leaning his cheek against her hair, he breathed in her familiar perfume. It mingled pleasantly with the scent of spruce and holly. "I don't guess it gets much better than this, does it?"

Her sigh was pure contentment. "We'll probably say the same thing next year. It'll be the baby's first Christmas."

Andy hoped there would be some other changes next year. He wanted to be married, to have their future completely settled. Next Christmas, he intended for them to be a family in every sense of the word, in the traditional sense. He worried sometimes, afraid he was living in a fool's paradise. Because everything with Meg was so right these days. They didn't make promises to each other. They didn't talk about remarriage. But underneath, there was something strong, a sense that they were moving, at long last, in the right direction.

Every day Andy fell deeper in love with her.

He realized now that what he had felt for Meg when they were married was infatuation. Or deep, abiding lust, as Lisa might say. Those feelings weren't gone. Just thinking of Meg could still leave him with a hard physical ache. But there was more between them now, something bigger, richer, more complete. He wanted to grab hold of that feeling with both hands, to somehow make sure it would last. But he knew there were no guarantees when it came to tender emotions. So he accepted each day with Meg as a gift.

Thoughts of gifts made him smile. "I have something for you."

She sat up, her expression eager. "I thought you didn't believe in opening presents before Christmas morning."

"You're a bad influence."

"Oh, goody." She rubbed her hands together. "What is it?"

Andy went to the tree and made a great show of rummaging through the various gifts he had bought for her. Finally, when she began to protest, he pulled a small gold-foil-wrapped package from the branch where he had hung it.

"I didn't even know that was there."

"I sneaked it on this afternoon. Otherwise, I knew you'd be here shaking it to death." Settling on the floor next to her again, he dropped the package into her lap. "So open it."

She needed no encouragement. Inside the green velvet jeweler's box was a necklace made of delicate gold filigree. Two hearts, outlined in diamonds, swung in the center.

"I liked the two hearts," Andy explained. "They made me think of you and the baby. You see the way the bigger heart kind of cradles the smaller one?"

"I see." Meg felt tears burning her eyes as she looked up at Andy. He had given her jewelry before, beautiful jewelry. Her engagement ring had been exquisite, and for their first Christmas, he had worked extra duty in order to afford a much too expensive set of ruby earrings. But neither of those gifts had as much thought behind them as this one did. She doubted he would ever give her another gift that would mean as much. "We love it," she whispered finally. "Me and the baby."

Andy's grin was rather lopsided. "Boomer said you would."

At the sound of his name, the dog barked, diffusing the intensity of the mood that had settled over them. Meg laughed and patted the setter's russet head. "For that, I think this big puppy deserves a whole plate of Christmas cookies."

She wore the necklace to the midnight Christmas Eve services at the church she had attended as a child. The chapel was filled to capacity. Candles glowed in the stained glass windows. At the altar was a Nativity scene. Children—including her niece and nephews—dressed as shepherds and angels, were gathered around the manger in the same poses Meg and her brother and sister had assumed years ago, in the same spot where her own child might someday stand. That thought made her smile.

With Andy on one side and her parents on the other, she listened to the familiar story of the Christ child's birth. Together, the congregation lifted their voices in songs of reverence and joy. As they sang, the baby stirred in her womb, and Meg touched a hand to the delicate gold hearts resting at her throat. She sent up a special prayer for the baby, for its health and well-being. This child was fine. Nothing could happen to it. Even as she said the words to herself, she was gripped by panic and by a single ugly thought.

If anything happens to the baby, I'll lose Andy.

It was a horrible, selfish thing to think, a thought she regretted the moment it was formed. She loved the child she carried. She didn't doubt she would lay down her life to save it. Yet she gave in to the worry that was never far from her mind these days. It was the baby Andy wanted. Not her. Without the baby...

Taking a deep breath, she tried to take hold of her runaway thoughts. Music swirled around her, and beneath the hymn book she and Andy shared, his hand was warm against her own. This was the safest, most peaceful place she had ever known, the most joyful night of the year. Yet she couldn't shake her unease, her distress at having had such selfish thoughts. God, what kind of mother was she going to be, anyway?

Andy seemed to sense her panic. Close to her ear, he whispered, "What's wrong?"

She shook her head. She couldn't tell him. He would think she was a monster. She felt like a monster, as if she had betrayed her own child. Drawing on all her strength, she tried to put the troubling thoughts aside.

But in early January, when the contractions started—the much too early, unexpected contractions—she remembered that moment in the church. And she wondered if her selfishness was being punished.

Andy hated hospitals. Nothing good had ever happened to him there. In a hospital, he'd had to face the reality of his brother's death. It was in a hospital, the day after he'd been shot over eight years ago, that Meg had told him their marriage was over. But here he was again, racing through an emergency room, facing the impersonal glare of a harried young desk clerk.

"Is Meg Hathaway in here?"

"Are you a relative?"

"Her hus—" He paused, corrected himself, "I'm the father of her baby."

The woman scrutinized him for a second, then pressed a button to unlock the door between the waiting area and the examining rooms. "Through the door to your right. Examining room Ten."

As he quickly followed her directions, Andy tried to get his panic under control. He and Will had been out chasing down leads on a new case when the dispatcher sent a code, asking him to call in immediately. The message said Meg was in the hospital and needed him to come right away. Andy had been ready to chuck departmental regulations and run the siren all the way to the hospital. But Will had kept a cooler head and broken every speed record and several laws in getting Andy there.

Outside Meg's room, the woman Andy recognized as her secretary, Pamela, met him in the hall. But before she could explain anything, the doctor stepped into the hall.

"Is Meg okay?" Andy demanded.

Dr. Mellman looked at him blankly over the tops of her spectacles, then recognition dawned. "It's Andy, isn't it? We met during one of Meg's office visits. I think she's out of danger."

The word made Andy blink. "Danger?"

She opened the door and gestured for him to come inside. "Let's go in and talk with Meg."

Meg lay flat on an examining table. Her face was pale and streaked with tears, but she found a wan smile for Andy as she held out her hand to him. "I'm so glad to see you."

Taking her hand, he stooped to brush a kiss across her forehead. "What in the hell happened?"

The doctor explained. "She had some rather severe cramping this afternoon."

"And some spotting," Meg said, clutching his hand tighter. "I thought I was having the baby."

Andy's mouth went dry. "But it's way too early."

"About six weeks," Dr. Mellman agreed. "That's why I had Meg come straight in here. She was very upset—"

"Hysterical," Meg said ruefully. "I'm sure the entire office is still reeling from the display I put on. Pamela brought me over here."

The doctor smiled in reassurance. "Because you were so upset, I didn't waste time asking you to come to the office. If there was a problem, the best place for you to be was here."

"But it's okay now?" Andy asked. "Out in the hall you said she was out of danger."

"We think so. There've been no more contractions or spotting since she came in."

Meg managed a laugh. "I'm feeling fine, actually."

Dr. Mellman patted her on the arm. "That's good. It doesn't appear that anything major was going on.

The baby had dropped some since your last visit, but I don't believe you're in any immediate danger of delivering early. The cramping you experienced could have been some particularly strong Braxton Hicks contractions.''

Andy interrupted, ''What is that?''

''Braxton Hicks contractions,'' Dr. Mellman repeated. ''I'm sure Meg has told you about them. They're very slight contractions that a women feels from as early as the third month of pregnancy. Later, in the last few months, they become more pronounced. And if the woman overdoes or stays on her feet too long—'' she directed a reproving glance at Meg ''—it's possible they can become very painful. They may be what happened to Meg today.''

''But the spotting—''

''Is a concern,'' Dr. Mellman conceded. ''I want Meg to stay here for a little while longer. She can sit up, but I want her calm and thinking good thoughts about the baby.'' She looked hard at Meg again. ''And once we're sure you're out of danger, I want us to talk about you slowing down for the next month or so. Now, I'll be back in to check on you shortly.'' She nodded to Meg and to Andy and left, the door swinging shut behind her.

But before Andy or Meg could say anything, there was a soft knock on the door and Pamela came in. Eyes wide, she asked Meg, ''How are you?''

Meg released Andy's hand and pushed herself up on her elbows. ''The doctor says I'm okay. And Andy's here now. You can go on back to the office. Tell everyone I'm fine."

Pamela nodded. "I had someone cancel the rest of today's appointments. I'll take care of tomorrow's when I get back."

Meg sat the rest of the way up, her forehead creasing in a frown. "Call and try to reschedule the Crisman appointment for early next week. They've got some urgent problems."

"Next week is pretty tight."

"Work them in somehow. And see if someone else can talk with the Hastings controller tomorrow."

"And what about—"

At that point, Andy broke in, demanding of Meg, "What are you doing?"

"I have clients, Andy. I have to take care of them."

"You have to take care of our baby, too." He turned to Pamela. "Go back to the office, tell them she won't be there the rest of this week—at least. Tell them to handle things by themselves."

"She can't do that," Meg protested.

Obviously confused, her secretary sent an anxious glance between them.

Andy snapped, "Are you waiting for something?" And Pamela fled the room.

As the door swung shut, Meg glared at him. "You didn't have to bark at her that way."

His only response was another order. "I want you to lie down. I'm going out to tell Will what's going on. He'll have to get someone to bring my car over here so we can get home." As he went out the door, he tossed over his shoulder, "Lie down. And remember, Dr. Mellman said to stay calm."

Calm. Repeating the word, trying to focus on tranquil images of sandy beaches and lazy summer days, Meg lay back. But it was hard to be calm in the face of everything that had happened. She had been sure the baby was coming this afternoon. She had been terrified, thinking only of that moment on Christmas Eve when she had wondered how Andy would react if something happened to their child. She was far too sensible to really believe she was being punished for those thoughts. Yet she felt guilty. So incredibly, horribly guilty. And she was still so scared.

And Andy didn't help matters, talking to Pamela that way, making decisions for Meg, and in general, acting like the barbarian he used to be.

She lifted her head to protest again when he came barreling back into the room, but he didn't give her a chance. He announced, "You know you're going to have to stay home, don't you?"

It took her a moment to assimilate what he had said. "What are you talking about?"

"Like Dr. Mellman said, you've got to slow down."

"She said slow down, not stay home."

"I think it's the same thing."

Groaning, Meg lay her head back down on the table. "If you're going to stand around here giving me orders, I wish you'd leave."

"I'm not leaving. And you're going to listen to me."

She seized the remote control button with which the nurse could be summoned and pointed it at Andy like a gun. "I'm warning you. I don't want to hear this now. If you don't shut up, I'll call the nurse to throw you out." She didn't realize how her voice had risen until she heard it echo around the room.

Staring at her, square jawed but silent, Andy dropped into a chair near the door.

Meg squeezed her eyes shut and lay back again. "I've got enough to worry about without listening to any of that overbearing nonsense you used to pull on me years ago." She drew in a deep breath. "I thought we were past that kind of garbage. But I can see I was wrong. Here you are, ordering people around like some kind of little Hitler, while here I lie—" her voice broke, caught on a sob, while her hands clenched over her stomach "—here I lie, with this baby...our baby..."

She didn't realize Andy had left his chair until his hand closed over hers. "Shh," he murmured. "Don't, Meggy. Please don't cry." His other hand went to her hair. He stroked it back from her forehead.

Struggling with her tears, she looked up at him. His eyes were a deep, troubled blue. "You don't know what I felt like today. I was just sure..." Again she swallowed her tears. "I just knew..."

"Everything's going to be okay," Andy whispered. "I promise you. Our baby's going to be fine."

Meg couldn't help herself. She had to ask the question most on her mind, "What if she weren't okay? What if we lost her?"

He perched on the edge of the table and drew her up and into his arms. "That's not going to happen."

"But what if it did?" she insisted. "What would happen to us?"

"I don't know what you mean."

She spelled it out. "If we lost the baby, would we lose us, too?"

Leaning back, he gave her a searching look.

Meg's hands settled on the nubby tweed of his jacket's lapels. She focused on the red-and-gray stripes in his tie. If she looked directly at Andy, she would lose her nerve, she would never say what had to be said. "I don't want to lose you. Even if the baby..." She took a deep breath. "Even if we lost the baby, I want to keep trying, keep working on us."

With his fingertips, he lifted her face up to his. Tenderly he traced the outline of her lips. His voice was husky. "You're not going to lose me. Now that I've found you again, we're not going to lose each other." He smiled his cocky, arrogant smile. "I don't want any more talk about losing this baby or me. Is that understood?"

It wasn't the declaration of undying love she hoped for. But it was reassurance. So was the steady, non-threatening kick of the baby against the wall of her womb. "Feel," she said, drawing Andy's hand down to her stomach. "She's kicking up a storm."

He touched her, felt the movement of life beneath her skin. "Yeah, *he's* quite a boy."

The old argument made them smile into each other's eyes.

Dr. Mellman surprised them that way a few moments later. Stopping inside the door, she lowered her glasses and grinned. "Well, it looks to me as if everything is going much better in here."

Smiling at Andy, Meg said, "I really do feel fine."

"That's good to hear." The doctor flipped the chart she held shut. She fixed Meg with a stern glance. "But now it's time to get serious. I didn't like what I heard from you today. Granted you were scared when the contractions started, but you did become hysterical. The spotting worries me, and your blood pressure's slightly elevated. You seem really stressed out." She turned her gaze to Andy. "This woman needs to be looked after for a few weeks."

Before he could respond, Meg promised, "I'll slow down at the office. The baby is more important than anything else."

Dr. Mellman shook her head. "I don't think that's good enough, Meg. I think you should take some time off. In two weeks, if you feel well enough and there've been no more problems, you can go back to work—part-time—until the baby is born. But at the first sign of a problem, I want you in bed. You want a full-term baby, Meg. It's what's best for you and the child."

To Andy's credit, he didn't act superior. There wasn't even an I-told-you-so glance. He shook the doctor's hand and said, "I'm going to make sure she doesn't even think about the office for a few days."

With a little smile, Dr. Mellman said, "Then I'll leave her in your capable hands."

Breathing a sigh of relief, Andy started toward the door. "Let me see if my car's here and we'll go home." He paused, turned back to Meg. "And we're going to my house. Where there are no stairs to climb." His smile flashed again. "And that's an order."

Only a few hours later, Meg was installed in Andy's bedroom. Boomer, who seemed to sense all wasn't well, lay across the foot of the bed. Perri had called Meg's office, found out about the crisis and had already appeared with a stack of magazines, several books and the promise that she would visit tomorrow. The phone rang all night—Will, Lisa, Meg's parents and her boss.

Andy spent the night alternating between asking Meg how she was feeling and hooking up a VCR to the bedroom TV. She got him to stop long enough to watch her favorite television program, but even then he kept racing back and forth from the kitchen with a variety of snacks. Just watching him wore Meg out.

Finally, when he got up for perhaps the fiftieth time, she called a halt. "Come here, Lieutenant." She patted the bed next to her.

"I'm just going—"

"Now!"

He saluted. "Yes, ma'am." He sat down on the edge of the bed.

"No," she said, throwing back the covers. "I want you in this bed. I want the television off. The lights out. I want your arms around me. And I want us to go to sleep that way."

"I thought I'd sleep in the guest room."

"Andy, I feel fine. I'm not going to break in two." She patted her belly. "The baby doesn't want to sleep without you. I don't want to sleep without you." She pointed to the end of the bed. "Even Boomer doesn't want to sleep without you."

He smiled at her. "This is going to be a crowded bed."

"Shut up and turn out the lights."

As if in assent, Boomer gave a short little bark.

"That's doggy talk for get moving," Meg said, laughing.

In a matter of moments, she was snuggled in Andy's arms. And sometime after that, between the kiss he pressed to her neck and when her eyes began to droop, she thought she heard him say he loved her.

And even if those words were only a dream, they made her wake with a smile on her face.

Chapter Ten

With Jocelyn in her arms, Perri stood on Andy's front porch and gave Meg the once-over. "My, my, but don't we look like the lady of leisure."

Though shivering in the frigid January wind, Meg still managed to flush under her friend's scrutiny. She stepped back. "Oh, come in, before you and the baby freeze to death."

"I hope we didn't wake you."

They had, but Meg didn't want to admit it. It was eleven o'clock. By this time on any usual weekday, she would have had several appointments or spent hours poring over financial records or tax forms. This morning—in fact, for the past several mornings—she had stayed in her warm, comfortable bed after Andy left for work. She had sipped hot chocolate and watched all the morning talk shows, and today she had drifted back to sleep. That's why she now faced Perri's regard in a worn flannel robe.

Shifting the baby to one hip, Perri circled Meg. "Let's see, there's no smart little business outfit, no briefcase. And I forgot to check the driveway. Have you sold the BMW yet?"

"Ha-ha. Very funny." Holding out her arms, Meg took Jocelyn and pulled off the baby's woolen cap. "Jocey, your mother should give up mothering and be a comedian." The baby gurgled in response.

Perri dropped her diaper bag and parka onto the couch and sprawled there herself. "Believe me, today is one of those days when I would gladly be anything but a mother."

"I don't really believe that." Meg slipped the snow suit off Jocelyn and then hugged her close, breathing in the sweet, special baby scents—a combination of powder, juice and cereal.

"Just wait until Andy, Jr. is five," Perri said. "Just wait till he tells you—as my five-year-old told me this morning—that the reason the commode in the hall bathroom isn't working is because he stuffed modeling clay down it the day before yesterday."

Meg couldn't quite suppress her smile. "Maybe he was conducting an experiment. You know, to see how clay dissolves in water or something."

Perri glared at her. "You don't seem to understand, Meg. Four people are now sharing one bathroom. Once upon a time I could at least go to the bathroom and be alone. No more.''

"So call a plumber."

"And give up all hope of balancing the budget this month?''

"I'm sure you'll manage."

Jocelyn started fussing then, and with a sigh, Perri roused herself to dig through her diaper bag for a bottle. She went to the kitchen and heated it in the microwave.

With blissful dreams of her own baby, Meg sat down in Andy's gray leather recliner to give the baby her bottle. "Don't you miss breast feeding?" she asked Perri, who had resumed her previous position on the couch.

Her friend rolled her green eyes. "It was a wonderful experience. I gave all three of my kids a great start on a lifetime of immunities. But now I'm reclaiming my breasts, thank you. They've belonged to someone else long enough.''

For the first time, Meg saw beyond the laughter to the real unhappiness in her friend's face. "Is something bothering you, Perri?"

"Oh, how did you guess?"

"Cut the smart talk and tell me."

Propping her legs on the coffee table, Perri said, "I think I have to go back to work."

Distressed, Meg stared at her. "But that's horrible. Is it money? I thought things were going okay for Rod.''

"He's doing fine, but it takes a lot for a family of five. And besides, I want to go back. I'm going insane at home."

"You? The earth mother? Insane?"

"Don't look so shocked."

"But I am."

Perri ruffled a hand through her tangled red curls. "I loved being at home with the boys. I had fun with them. But now I'm tired. Tired of building blocks and kiddie videotapes. I know that's a terrible admission for a mother to make, but when I think of how much I still have to go through with Jocey here..." She shook her head. "I just don't know."

Meg looked down at the pretty baby girl in her arms. "So you're going to put her in day-care?"

Perri frowned. "That's what bothers me. I mean, I was home with the boys. I taught them to count, to say their names. I potty-trained them. They didn't start going to any kind of day-care until they were three. Now Chris is in kindergarten and Matt's in preschool, and I'm glad they're out of the house. I really believe they're better off being with other kids right now."

She smoothed a hand down her faded blue jeans. "When I get up in the mornings to take them to school, I'd like to put on some heels and a suit and go off to a job. And if things had worked out, if little Jocey hadn't popped into our lives..." Her eyes grew round with distress. "Oh, God, Meg, you know we wouldn't trade her for the world."

"I know."

"But if things had gone according to plan, I could go back to work now with a pretty clear conscience. As it is, she'll be in day-care and someone else will teach her all the things I taught the boys." She groaned. "God, that makes me feel guilty as hell."

"But millions of women face this," Meg said. "It isn't a choice for most of them." *I'm going to do it,* she added silently. But the thought hit her with the same peculiar pang it had produced in recent days. Maybe it was all this forced inactivity, but she had been thinking about what she was going to miss by going off to work every day.

"Are you still going to hire someone to be with the baby at home?" Perri asked.

Meg nodded. "I think that'll work out for the best. The baby won't have to get out on cold mornings. The nanny will be right there when the baby's sick. I won't have to miss work. And I've already got names of some good people to check out. It'll be fine." But it didn't feel fine. Even though she was so much luckier than many mothers, because she could afford to hire some full-time help, it still didn't feel right.

"Uh-huh."

Perri's soft sound made Meg glance up. "What?"

"You don't really want a nanny, do you?"

She lied, "Sure I do. It's the only way."

Her friend still looked skeptical. "And what does Andy want?"

"He's leaving this up to me."

"Really?" Perri's eyebrows climbed another notch. "I'm surprised. He's been so involved in everything else, so far. I figured he'd be the one to interview prospective nannies."

"I think he's planning to do a security check on them."

"Figures." Glancing around the room, Perri asked, "Where are you guys going to live, anyway?"

"At my place, of course. That's where the nursery is."

"And when is the wedding?"

"There isn't a wedding being planned."

"Not yet, anyway."

"Perri, Andy hasn't said anything about getting married again."

"So ask him."

"After the fit I pitched the last time *he* asked? Puhlease."

Her friend sat forward. "Everything has changed since the last time he asked."

Meg bit her lip. "Maybe."

"Oh, come on. He's crazy about you. You're crazy about him. You were always in love. It's just taken you a while—a long while, I admit—to get it all worked out. You should get married before the baby is born."

Laughing, Meg slipped the nearly-empty bottle from Jocelyn and shifted the sleeping child into a more comfortable position. That wasn't easy to find since her stomach took up most of her lap, but she was reluctant to relinquish the baby. "I'd make a great-looking bride, wouldn't I?"

"That doesn't matter."

With her old friend, Meg could let some of her worries show. "I don't know, Perri. You would think Andy and I would look at each other, say we're in love and march down to city hall or something. But it doesn't happen."

"Like I said before, why don't you ask him?"

"Maybe I'm afraid he'd say no."

Perri blew out an exasperated breath. "That's crazy."

"It would seem that way," Meg agreed. "I mean, Andy is so great to me. All this week, he's taken such good care of me. He actually took two days off from work."

"Mr. Dedication took time off? I am impressed."

"I think he really has changed. His priorities are in order."

"You've changed, too."

"Yeah," Meg agreed. "I have."

Perri smiled at her. "Here you are, sitting in your robe on a workday, and you don't even look as though you mind."

"I don't."

"And you've actually let Andy take care of you. That's a first."

Meg smiled, thinking of the meals he had served her in bed, the funny and sweet cards he had left on his pillow every morning since he had returned to work. Sheepishly she admitted, "I sort of like being pampered."

Perri sat up straight, clutching her hands over her heart theatrically. "Oh, my God, you can't mean it?

Can this really be Meg Hathaway speaking, the girl so liberated she wouldn't allow dates in college to buy her a meal?''

"Oh, stop it," Meg declared. "You've been telling me for years that I needed to stop thinking I had to conquer the world on my own."

"The thing is, you can still conquer the world. You just don't have to come home to an empty house at night."

Perri was right, of course. She had been right all along. As Andy had stood beside her during this pregnancy, Meg had learned that leaning on someone didn't make her weak. Independence and freedom didn't necessarily exclude a loving, sharing relationship. Knowing how to combine all those elements was true liberation. And Meg thought she and Andy had a chance for that now. All of the pieces were ready to fall into place. If only they could make a final commitment to each other.

Sighing, Meg again looked down at the child she held. "Yes, little Jocey, don't you ever forget we women can have it all."

"Your mother always told us that," Perri reflected. "Remember, she said our generation would have all the choices we could ever want. She said nobody would ever try to hold us back."

Gently Meg stroked Jocelyn's silky fire-hued hair. "I wish Mother had been able to explain how hard these choices were going to be."

The two friends sighed in unison.

"I have a terrible confession to make," Meg said. "The last few days I've been fantasizing about calling up my boss and telling him I won't be back."

Perri sucked in her breath. "Walking out on a vice presidency? Meg..."

"I know. I know. I said it was a fantasy."

But Meg knew Perri could tell she had been giving this some serious thought. "Don't do anything until you've thought about this carefully. You've been working toward this job for a long time. Can you give up the dream? Give up the money?"

"I can always go back to work. But my baby will only be a baby once."

"Listen to the voice of experience, now. It isn't easy to stay home. There are days when you question your ability to carry on a conversation with anyone over the age of four."

"But Rod has always been so supportive of you staying home. He never seemed to diminish your job the way we've heard other husbands do."

"Oh, he's great," Perri confirmed. "He loves me. He loves our kids. But there are nights when he comes home and I hand them all to him. And that's not fair because he's had a rough day, too. So we end up with this strain between us and I start to think, why did I ever want this life?"

"You didn't want that life," Meg reminded her. "You were going to be a world-famous journalist."

Laughing, Perri nodded. "Then I ran into Rod in the cafeteria at school."

"And somewhere over mopping up spilled soda, you fell in love."

"Funny how these accidents will happen."

Meg patted her stomach. "Yes, it is funny, isn't it?"

"Oh, heavens," Perri said, standing up to stretch. "You and I could debate this whole thing for hours. Days, even. But you have to decide what's best for you, Meg. For you and the baby. And Andy, too. And speaking of you and Andy." She grinned, her eyes twinkling with excitement. "Lisa and I have been talking...."

"Lisa? You two talk?"

"After getting together a couple of times with you and Andy, she and I discovered we have lots in common. Little boys and good friends, in particular. We want to throw you guys a baby party."

"Party?"

"Sort of like a baby shower, but for couples. We want to wait until you're feeling up to it." Perri eyed Meg's stomach. "However, it is customary to have these things before the mother delivers. And from the size of you, that could be any time."

"Go ahead, make fun of how big I am," Meg told her. "I know you're getting back at me for all those blimp jokes I made during your pregnancies."

"Paybacks are hell, aren't they?"

"You're a one-in-a-million friend, Perri." The words were said only half in jest. For Meg realized how special it was that her friendship with this woman had lasted so long, that it still remained strong and honest. No matter what, she could always count on Perri.

The redhead's eyes were suspiciously moist as she smiled at Meg. "Come on, if we get sentimental and start crying now, we'll never get this party planned. I need some names and addresses. And you haven't heard the best part—Lisa and I think we should use *your* condo for this. I mean, you have the quintessential party house. This will be the baby shower to end all baby showers."

She was right, as usual.

By the next weekend, Lisa and Perri had put together a fabulous party. Great food, of course. And an eclectic mix of guests. Andy stood to the side in Meg's living room, watching his family and friends mingle with Meg's. Her mother, the college economics professor, was talking drug busts with his Captain. Meg's father and his were across the room, sharing a drink and a cigar. Andy had cousins in attendance that he hadn't seen in years. Meg's boss, who was fiftyish and divorced, had been flirting with Lisa all night, while Will stood watching them, a beer in his hand, pretending not to care. Studying his partner's usually inscrutable features, Andy decided Meg was right. She had told him last week that there was something going on between Will and Lisa. They might not even know it themselves, but it was there, nevertheless.

Andy shook his head and to no one in particular said, "I don't think this is your usual baby shower."

Lisa, who was passing by with a replenished platter of goodies, answered him, "Why are you surprised? You and Meg aren't the usual expectant parents."

"How's that?"

The blonde grinned at him. "I could list perhaps a dozen reasons, starting with the fact that you're divorced...*still* divorced."

Andy didn't miss the emphasis Lisa put on her words. She had been razzing him for weeks about asking Meg to marry him. "All right, Lisa, cut it out. You're feeling extra cocky tonight. And we both know why."

Glancing around, she lowered her voice and gloated, "Well, there is a certain investigation, one you and everyone else told me to forget, an arson case, an accidental death that I'm about to prove was more..."

"Okay, okay, don't get cocky. I'm the only one who can be a hotshot, you know."

Lisa sniffed and turned to go. Over her shoulder, she said, "Just remember, *my* instincts are pretty darn good, too. And right now, I have a hunch about a certain person saying yes to a certain very overdue question."

At that moment, Meg slipped a hand through Andy's arm. "What are you two cops talking about?"

He flushed. Lisa giggled and moved across the room.

"You're keeping secrets from me," Meg said.

Andy patted her hand. "Lisa's about to crack a case she's been working on for a while. It's supposed to go down tomorrow. I forgot to tell you I'll be in on it. I know it's the weekend, but I'll have to go in tomorrow."

Frowning, Meg searched his face. "It isn't dangerous, is it?"

"You shouldn't worry."

That was really no answer, but Meg stilled her impatience. She had learned that Andy couldn't, wouldn't tell her everything. She had to trust him on that.

Above the buzz of conversation, she heard her name being called and looked up. It was her boss. "I was wondering," he said. "Have you guys settled on a name for the baby?"

The room grew quiet while Meg looked uncertainly at Andy. There were names they had discussed, but did he want them announced, here, like this? His nod, the gentle pressure of his hand on hers said yes.

"Well, I got my way about hyphenating the baby's last name," she said, smiling up at Andy. "So I thought it would be appropriate to let the first name be something that's special to Andy." Her gaze went to Andy's parents, who were now standing together across the room. "If it's a boy, we're going to name him David. For Andy's brother."

As expected, Lucy cried. Even Karl looked pleased as he patted his wife's arm. And as an explanation of what had happened to David sped around the room, there were some other eyes that grew suspiciously moist.

In the general hubbub, Meg couldn't make herself heard until finally she raised her voice. "Doesn't anyone want to hear the girl's name?'' Conversation died, and again she looked straight at Andy's father. "If it's a girl, she'll be Karla—with a *K* of course, for her grandfather."

There was a round of applause for that. But Karl said nothing at first. Then, as the party noises began to swell again, he made his way slowly across the room. Meg stood to the side while father and son faced each other.

She didn't expect any great emotional scene. That was too much to hope for. It was enough that Andy put out his hand. She was proud of him for that. For it showed he had truly learned there was something to be gained by reaching out to someone else. The fact that Karl took that hand, that he smiled at his son, proved that it was never too late for a family to heal.

Never too late.

The words kept chasing around in Meg's mind the next morning while she sat in bed, stroking Boomer's sleek coat and watching Andy strap his shoulder holster on over his gray sweatshirt. Nearly nine months ago, she'd thought it *was* too late for her and Andy. But in a few weeks, they would have a child. And they had a future together. It was astounding the way life could turn around.

Andy put a denim jacket on and turned from the dresser mirror to smile at her. "You look very content this morning."

"I'm happy."

He crossed the bed and bent to kiss her. "I'm happy, too."

Grasping the lapels of his jacket, she held him close to her for a minute. She could feel his gun pressing through the denim. "Be careful today."

Lightly he brushed his knuckles across her jaw. "Tonight, when I come home, I want us to make some decisions."

"Oh?"

"Big decisions."

She thought she knew what those decisions might be. And the thought warmed her. "I'll be waiting."

He turned to go, but he paused in the doorway, looking back at Meg. Weak winter sunlight filtered through the window, bringing out the shine in her ebony hair. And even now, in the last stage of pregnancy, in a high-necked, prim flannel nightgown, she was the most desirable woman he had ever known. He was determined she was going to marry him this week.

It was Meg Andy thought about that morning while he met with Lisa and Will and several other officers to go over today's plan. It wasn't like him to be so distracted. But Meg and the coming baby had changed him forever. He might have been a hotshot once, but now he just wanted to do the job. He wanted to do it right, of course. He still cared, still wanted to make a difference. But now he had something special to live for, someone he loved, a child to raise.

Later that afternoon, when everything started to go horribly, terribly wrong, it was Meg and the baby that Andy thought of first.

And his hesitation cost him, cost him dearly.

Chapter Eleven

Meg wanted to run. But just walking these days required a great deal of balance. So she hurried, moving as fast as she could down the blandly painted hospital corridors. Perspiration beaded her forehead, and her heart was pounding when she rounded the corner and went into the intensive care unit's waiting room.

She found Will sitting in a chair in the corner, his head buried in his hands. A jacket lay on the floor beside him. Andy's jacket, Meg thought, though she didn't know why it mattered. Then Will looked up and saw her, his expression so tortured, so shattered, she immediately assumed the worst.

"My God!" she exclaimed. "Where's Andy?"

Will jerked his thumb toward the set of double doors at the other end of the room. "He's in with Lisa. They tried throwing him out, saying no one was allowed in intensive care except for family. But he made such a commotion, they let him stay. And of course, Lisa has no family, except for Terry, so I guess it's right that Andy should be with her. He's her best friend."

"What about Terry?" Meg asked, her heart aching for Lisa's little boy. "Does he know?"

"She always leaves his sitter's number with the dispatcher. The Captain and his wife know Terry—their son goes to school with him, so they've gone over to tell him. I mean, nobody wants to scare the little guy, but he has to know...in case." Will took a deep breath. "In case the worst happens. I thought maybe Terry should be here, but Andy said no. He doesn't think Lisa would want him to see her this way."

Meg nodded. It was a tough call. But she knew Andy would know what Lisa would want.

"Just exactly how bad is she?" Meg asked. "There wasn't time to discuss it on the phone."

"She took a bullet in the chest. It just missed her heart. There's a lot of damage to her lung. She's not breathing on her own right now."

Closing her eyes against the horror of one of her worst fears, Meg put her hand against the wall for support. She had known something was wrong when evening arrived and Andy still hadn't called her. In the past few weeks, he *always* called. But seven had arrived, then eight, and she had begun to panic. She was about to call the precinct office when Will called her.

Will's touch on her arm made her open her eyes. He guided her into a chair. "Damn, Meg, you shouldn't have come running over here. When I called, I just wanted you to know. You're supposed to still be taking it easy, aren't you?"

She brushed his concerns aside. "When did this happen? You said on the phone that they had already done emergency surgery on her."

"It was early afternoon when she was shot."

"Early afternoon? Then why hasn't Andy called me?"

Leaning against the wall, Will pressed the heels of his hands against his eyes. "He's taking this hard, Meg. Real hard. I mean, he's gonna be mad as hell when he finds out I called you, but I thought maybe you should know."

"Of course I should know."

"Andy's blaming himself."

"But why?"

Will sank into the chair beside hers with an exhausted sigh. "You know good old first-one-through-the-door Baskin. Lisa got ahead of him this time, so he thinks he's responsible for what happened."

"That's crazy."

"Yeah, irrational. The whole damn thing is crazy."

Meg stood and started toward the ICU doors. "I'm going in to him."

"Good luck in getting past the nurses in there. They're pretty tough."

"And I'm determined." At the doors, Meg looked back over her shoulder. Will's head was in his hands again. He seemed so devastated. "Hey," she said softly. He looked up. "You care about her, don't you?"

His dark eyes narrowed. "Yeah. I care."

"Then pray. That's all we can do now."

Meg pushed through the doors and found herself in a hallway where still another set of doors led to the ICU. She wondered at the arrangement. It made her think of limbo, the place that some religions regarded as a region that bordered on hell. But perhaps the hall was appropriate, because in some respects the room behind the second set of doors could be regarded as hell.

The space was circular in design, with the nurses' station in the center and glass-fronted patient cubicles lining the perimeter. There was a hushed sense of urgency here. A prevailing sadness. Voices were quiet. Lights blinked on sophisticated-looking equipment.

A young male nurse looked up from the chart he held and frowned at Meg. "ICU visiting hours are over. The times are posted on the doors."

"But I have to see Lisa Talbot."

"Are you family?"

"Her sister," Meg lied, and when the nurse looked skeptical, she added, "Sister-in-law."

He hesitated only a moment more, then gestured to one of the cubicles at the far side of the circle. Meg went around the nurses' station. Through a glass partition, she saw Andy. He sat in a chair beside a bed.

Meg paused outside the door. Lisa was barely visible beneath the maze of tubes and wires. Meg recognized the sound of the steady beep-beep of the heart monitor. At least that sound was steady. She thanked God for that much.

Andy didn't even look up when she went in the room. She finally had to say his name to get his attention. Ashen faced, he didn't seem to recognize her at first. Meg went toward him, touched his arm. "How is she?"

"She's not coming around."

"Will said she hadn't been out of surgery too long. Perhaps it's too early for her to come to."

Andy shook his head. "The doctors aren't giving me any reasons. But they don't look too happy."

Heart aching for him, Meg slipped an arm around his shoulders. "It seems to me doctors are always being pessimistic. They never want to get anyone's hopes up."

Andy shrugged, his gaze not wavering from Lisa's white, still features.

"Do you want to tell me what happened?" she asked quietly.

"It doesn't matter."

"It might help to talk about it."

He didn't even reply.

"Why don't you step out of here for a while?"

He shook his head. "I want to be here if she comes to."

"I'll stay with her, come and get you if anything happens."

But again his reply was negative.

Meg tried once more. "I'm sure you're hungry. Come down to the cafeteria and get something to eat with me. Will wants to come in and see Lisa."

Arms braced on the chair's aluminum-barred sides, Andy leaned forward, resting his chin on his steepled fingers. "I don't want to leave her."

Meg thought she understood. He was in shock and filled with guilt—however mistaken that guilt was. He probably thought something horrible would happen if Lisa was out of his sight. So Meg pulled the room's other chair close to his and they sat, silently, watching her.

When ICU's regular visiting period came, Meg went out and sent Will in. Andy wouldn't budge. She finally went down to the cafeteria and got him a sandwich and a cup of coffee.

The hours stretched from two into three. The doctor came and went, reporting no change in Lisa's condition. The Captain came by and reported that Terry was at his house, very upset but trying hard to be brave. Meg thought about going to the child, but somehow she thought Andy needed her more. She rotated from Lisa's room to the waiting area, where she finally got Will to tell her exactly what had happened.

She remembered Lisa talking about the case—a fire in an unfinished office building. Two of the development company's principals, the sister and son of the firm's president, had died in the blaze. It was clearly arson. And even though the reasons why they would want to burn the building down were never found, it had been assumed the two people who perished had been setting the fire. Lisa had a hunch they'd been murdered. The forensic report was inconclusive, so there was no real evidence to support her intuition. The only thing she had to go on was the uneasy feeling she'd had after questioning the company president, a Mr. Jay Hastings.

"But last week, she got a new lead," Will explained. "One of the company's most senior employees came to Lisa and said he thought Hastings had planned the whole fire, including the murder. It seems Hastings has been acting erratically for the last few weeks, drinking too much, carrying on about his son. He said something that tipped this employee off. Maybe he didn't plan on his son dying, maybe the two of them were in on the scheme together."

Meg shivered. "Why would they do it?"

"The most obvious motive is greed. Maybe Hastings and his son wanted control of the company themselves and decided to knock off the sister. They probably hoped the arson and fire would cover the evidence. But it went wrong and the son died, too. Unless there was someone else in on the scheme, I guess we'll never know."

"Why not?"

Will stared at her in surprise. "I thought I told you."

"Told me what?"

"The guy... Hastings... he's dead." Will dropped his hand to cover hers. "Andy killed him, right after Hastings shot Lisa."

Andy killed him.

While those words chased around and around in her head, Meg sucked in her breath. No wonder Andy was in the outer limits of despair. Not only was Lisa lying near death. He'd had to take another man's life. And no matter what the reason, she knew he wouldn't take that lightly.

"I'm sorry, Meg, for some reason..." Will slumped back in his chair. "Hell, I don't know what I've said to who today."

"There are still things I don't understand," Meg said. "Why did Hastings shoot Lisa?"

Will explained that Lisa had questioned Hastings after his employee came in with his suspicions. But Hastings's story didn't waver from the one he had told right after the fire. He said he knew nothing about why the fire was set or why his sister and son were on the scene. He had an alibi in his own wife. Lisa still didn't believe he was telling the whole truth, but she needed some proof. The informant agreed to wear a wire, to try and elicit a confession from Hastings. It was a dangerous setup, but the informant was willing to try.

The two men had set up a meeting at a construction site, on the pretense that the informant wanted to go over some problems on a Sunday, when no one else was around. Surveillance equipment was put in place. The informant led the conversation around to the fire. But Hastings got suspicious and pulled a gun on him. Andy, Will, Lisa and other officers were on the scene to prevent such a tragedy.

"Lisa got there first," Will said, his hands clenching into fists on the arms of his chair. He shut his eyes. "Hastings shot her instead of his employee. Andy's bullet probably saved the other guy's life."

Meg's head drooped forward. Her voice sounded faint, faraway, even to her own ears. "And Andy thinks it's all his fault."

"And it wasn't." Will got to his feet and paced away, shaking his head. "Everyone who was there agrees. Lisa was closest to the action. Andy reacted in the only way he could have. Whichever one of them had gotten there first would have probably been hit."

And it could be Andy lying in that hospital bed.

Propelled by that horrible thought, Meg stood. "I have to talk to him about this. If he just sits there and broods, this thing will fester inside him. I know how he is. And if Lisa dies..." Not even bothering to look back at Will, she went to Lisa's room once more.

But Andy wouldn't talk to her.

She begged. She pleaded. Yet he shut her out, as he used to do.

Finally, exhausted, she allowed Will to drive her home. But she returned the next morning with fresh clothes and toiletries for Andy. He left Lisa long enough to grab a shower in the facilities the hospital provided for patients' families. But then he went right back to her side.

And he wouldn't discuss what had happened.

For three days, he and Meg reached the same impasse time and time again.

Andy finally stopped even listening to Meg. He couldn't look at her. Every time she walked into Lisa's room, he kept thinking of the moment when Hastings had pulled his gun. Andy had hesitated a second too long. In that instant, that flash of an eye, he had thought of Meg and the baby. He was certain that if he hadn't hesitated, Lisa wouldn't be fighting for her life. Throughout his career, in any crisis, he had always taken the lead. This time, he hadn't. It didn't matter what everyone else said, he *knew* this was his fault.

Finally, on the morning of the fourth day after the shooting, Meg couldn't stand his cold rejection of her any longer. She couldn't help it. She felt betrayed by Andy's reaction. She knew it wasn't fair to judge the strength of their relationship during such a tragedy, but she couldn't stop feeling as if all the progress they had made was now somehow invalidated. And as was usual, she went to Perri for comfort.

Perri let her cry it out. She sat silently by while Meg railed against Andy. Then she grasped Meg's shoulders and gave her a little shake.

"This isn't helping him, Meg."

"He won't let me help him. That's the point. It's like it always was before. He's shut me out."

Perri's eyes flashed with anger. "The man is grieving, Meg. Will says he thinks it's his fault. Have you considered the possibility that he can't talk about it yet?"

"But he should be able to tell me. I could help him." Hands on her stomach, where her baby stirred, she turned away from Perri. "I feel as if Andy is turning his back on me."

"That's silly."

Meg faced her friend again, filled with frustration and anger. "Maybe it is silly. But I think a person's true nature comes out when there's a crisis. And life is a series of crises. If this is the way Andy is going to react every time something happens..." She pressed a hand to her mouth, fighting back a fresh rush of tears. "That's not the kind of relationship I want."

"And you think relationships are built in a few months?" Perri demanded.

"Andy and I have been working on this for years."

Her friend shook her head. "No, you played at working it out for years. The real work has only come recently. It took this baby to make both of you give this a real try."

Meg shook her head. "I think I would have eventually realized how much I loved Andy, how much I wanted a relationship with him, even without the baby." The fear that had haunted her for months seemed to smack her in the face. "No matter what Andy says, the only thing that holds him to me is the baby. That much is obvious now."

Hands on hips, Perri glared at her. "I don't know which of you is more screwed up. Because if you can't see the love Andy has for you..." She shook her head. "He's been proving it over and over these past few months."

"For the baby's sake."

"I don't believe that," Perri said firmly. "And I think if you look deep in your own heart, you'll realize you don't believe it, either."

Meg yearned to agree with her friend, but something held her back. "If he loves me so much, why won't he let me help him now?"

"If you love *him* so much, why aren't you down at that hospital, by his side. When you really love someone, you keep going back, no matter how hard that person pushes you away."

As she stared at Perri, Meg realized something. All through the years, every time she and Andy had come together and then separated again, it was him who always came after her. She had always accused him of not being able to reach out. But he had. Time and time again. Oh, he might have been offering passion more than love. But he *had* tried to reach her. In the only way he could. And she had pushed him away.

It wasn't just the baby that held the two of them together. It was the feelings they had known from the start. Those emotions were stronger now, tested by time and separation. The feelings had a name. Love.

As that realization hit her, she hugged Perri. "Thanks, friend. I don't know what I'd do without you to set me straight every once in a while."

Perri sank down in one of her kitchen chairs. "I hope this is your last crisis for a while."

"I hope so, too. I'll call you from the hospital if there's any change in Lisa's condition."

Heart soaring with determination, Meg left for the hospital. This was one time she was going to wait Andy out.

The world outside the glass-enclosed ICU cubicle had almost ceased to exist for Andy. His joints were sore from sleeping in the chair next to Lisa's bed. And even in those fitful bouts of rest, he could hear the beep and squeaks of the equipment helping Lisa fight for her life.

He hoped they were helping. Andy didn't know if he would ever forgive himself if she spent the rest of her life this way. At least she was breathing on her own. Now if only Lisa would wake up.

The doctors said they weren't sure why she wasn't coming around. They were calling the emergency surgery that repaired her lung a success. It was all up to Lisa now. She had to find the strength to pull herself out of this.

Scooting his chair closer to her bed, he took her hand. Her skin was cool and dry. She didn't respond to his touch, but he held on to her regardless. The nurses had told him to talk to her. He had done so last night until he was hoarse. Even now his voice came out in a cracked whisper. "Wake up, Lisa. Please wake up. For Terry's sake. Wake up."

The only response was the sound of her heart monitor.

Andy bent forward, his head resting against the bed's cold steel side rails. "I wish I could go back," he said again. "I wish it were Sunday again. I promise you I wouldn't let this happen."

It was the same sort of one-sided conversation Andy used to conduct with the memory of his brother. He knew it was a useless exercise. None of them could ever turn back the clock. They had to keep looking forward. He had learned that with Meg. She had helped him see he couldn't spend the rest of his life trying to make up for the past. But that didn't seem so easy with Lisa lying here like this.

He lifted his head, stared hard at her unmoving features. "I've got to tell you something, Lisa. I don't know if I can live with my guilt over this. Not just that you got hit. That's bad enough. But there's something else. Something I didn't realize until I sat here talking to you last night."

He drew a shuddering breath. "You see, Lisa...even though I've been telling you and everyone else that I wish it were me in this bed, that's not true."

Moisture collected in his eyes, but he shook it off. "The real truth is that I'm damned glad that bullet didn't hit me. I didn't want to get shot. I realized that when I hesitated out there. For a whole lot of years, probably ever since I saw David die, my life has felt pretty expendable. That's why I was such a hotshot, why I took chances. I didn't think it mattered much to anyone if I lived or died."

His hand gripped Lisa's shoulder. "But that's not true anymore. Because Meg cares if I live. And our baby..." He shut his eyes. "Well, Lisa, you of all people know the real truth...there's nothing more important to me than Meg. Not the baby. Not this damn job. Not anything. She means everything to me. That's what I really realized out there the other day. That's why I'm so damned happy it's not me in this bed.''

Laying his head against the steel rails again, he said, ''I wish you'd wake up, Lisa. Right now. Because I'm going to take your advice. I'm going to find Meg. I'm going to tell her how much I love her. And if I haven't pushed her away one too many times, we're going to get married. It'd be kind of nice if you could make it to the wedding.''

A soft choking sound brought his head up. Lisa's lips were moving as if she were trying to speak. And her fingers stirred in his.

A rush of pure joy sent Andy to his feet. ''Lisa?''

She opened her eyes and looked at him. The lashes fluttered, but her gaze seemed to focus. Her voice was thin, a reedy almost unintelligible whisper, but he heard it nevertheless.

He bent forward. ''What is it?''

''Go...to...Meg.'' The words came out slowly, but a tiny smile twitched the corners of Lisa's mouth. ''Tell her... I want to catch the bouquet.''

Realizing he should be calling the nurse, Andy disregarded the button on the side of the bed and raised his voice instead. In only seconds, two nurses came running. But Lisa continued to cling to his hand. ''I have to...thank you, Andy. For once...you let...me be the hotshot.''

The sentiment was pure Lisa. It proved she was all right. Laughing with relief and happiness, Andy dropped her hand and stepped out of the nurses' way. Turning, he saw Meg.

She stood inside the door. Tears streaming down her face. Her arms open wide.

Andy stepped right into them. Gratefully he held on tight. And even though doctors and nurses pushed them out of ICU so that Lisa could be attended to, he didn't let go of Meg's hand.

In the corridor that ran between the two sets of double doors, he began an apology, "Meg, I'm so sorry—"

She put her hands to his lips. "No, I'm sorry. I should have been here with you."

"I shut you out."

"I let you."

"Oh, God." He caught her close, felt the baby moving inside her. "Meg, there's so much I want to say to you."

"I think I already heard it."

He drew away. "You heard me talking to Lisa?"

"Every word." Tears trembled on her eyelashes, fell to her cheeks. "I love you, Andy Baskin. I think I realized today that I always have."

He cupped her face in his hands. "I meant everything I said in there. You are my everything. You always will be."

They shared a kiss. Achingly sweet. All too brief.

Then Meg pulled Andy toward the other set of doors. They were going in the right direction this time.

Toward a future. "Come on, Terry and Will and everyone else are waiting for word on Lisa."

Andy tugged her back, wanting one more kiss.

But Meg didn't oblige. Instead, smiling up at him, she said, "Come on, Hotshot. We've got the rest of our lives for kissing."

Epilogue

Gathered in the doorway of the hospital room, there was a crowd. A giggling group. Meg let her gaze travel fondly over each of their faces. Lisa, who after two weeks in the hospital was looking as beautiful as ever. Will, who was at the helm of Lisa's wheelchair and, Meg suspected, her heart. And Perri, whose green eyes were even brighter than normal.

Then there was Andy.

Meg saved her fondest glance for him, this man she loved, who was the object of all the laughter. For he sat in a chair, cradling a precious bundle and cooing like a dove.

Stretching happily, Meg savored the sight of her husband and their child. Three days ago, she and

Andy had remarried in a small ceremony here in the hospital chapel so that Lisa could be with them. Yesterday, Meg had gone into labor.

So much had changed. Was it only nine months ago, she had stood in front of a mirror and wished for this kind of happiness? It seemed more like a lifetime ago. Now she had it all. The thought made her smile deepen. For in having it all, she knew she had a new set of problems. A new set of titles. Wife and mother had joined vice president and career woman. She wasn't sure if she was up to all these challenges. She might still have to make some hard choices. With Andy at her side, she felt downright invincible.

"So what do you think?" she asked him.

Somewhat reluctantly, he tore his gaze away from their baby. And he grinned. A typically Andy, typically cocky grin. "I think I always knew it would be a girl," he declared.

There were jeers from the onlookers.

And laughter from Meg. She snuggled down in the covers, content to watch Karla Hathaway-Baskin wrap her daddy around her tiny little finger.

* * * * *

This is the season of giving, and Silhouette proudly offers you its sixth annual Christmas collection.

SILHOUETTE

Christmas Stories

1991

Experience the joys of a holiday romance and treasure these heart-warming stories by four award-winning Silhouette authors:

Phyllis Halldorson—"A Memorable Noel"
Peggy Webb—"I Heard the Rabbits Singing"
Naomi Horton—"Dreaming of Angels"
Heather Graham Pozzessere—"The Christmas Bride"

Discover this yuletide celebration—sit back and enjoy Silhouette's Christmas gift of love.

Silhouette Special Edition

COMING NEXT MONTH

#709 LURING A LADY—Nora Roberts
Barging into his landlord's office, angry carpenter Mikhail Stanislaski got what he wanted. But, for the hot-blooded artist, luring cool, reserved landlady Sydney Hayward to his SoHo lair was another story....

#710 OVER EASY—Victoria Pade
Lee Horvat went undercover to trap Blythe Coopersmith by gaining her trust. She gave it too freely, though, and both were caught . . . struggling against love.

#711 PRODIGAL FATHER—Gina Ferris
It wasn't wealthy, stoic Cole Saxon's wish to reunite with his prodigal father; it was A-1 wish-granter Kelsey Campbell's idea. And from the start, Kelsey proved dangerously adept at directing Cole's desires....

#712 PRELUDE TO A WEDDING—Patricia McLinn
Paul Monroe was a top-notch appraiser. Sensing million-dollar laughter behind Bette Wharton's workaholic ways, he betrayed his spontaneous nature and planned . . . for a march down the aisle.

#713 JOSHUA AND THE COWGIRL—Sherryl Woods
Cowgirl Traci Garrett didn't want anything to do with big shots like businessman Joshua Ames. But that was before this persistent persuader decided to rope—and tie—this stubborn filly.

#714 EMBERS—Mary Kirk
Disaster summoned Anne Marquel home to face the ghosts of the past. With tender Connor McLeod's help, could she overcome tragedy and fan the embers of hope for tomorrow?

AVAILABLE THIS MONTH:

SILHOUETTE® OFFICIAL SWEEPSTAKES RULES

NO PURCHASE NECESSARY

1. To enter, complete an Official Entry Form or 3" × 5" index card by hand-printing, in plain block letters, your complete name, address, phone number and age, and mailing it to: Silhouette Fashion A Whole New You Sweepstakes, P.O. Box 9056, Buffalo, NY 14269-9056.

   No responsibility is assumed for lost, late or misdirected mail. Entries must be sent separately with first class postage affixed, and be received no later than December 31, 1991 for eligibility.

2. Winners will be selected by D.L. Blair, Inc., an independent judging organization whose decisions are final, in random drawings to be held on January 30, 1992 in Blair, NE at 10:00 a.m. from among all eligible entries received.

3. The prizes to be awarded and their approximate retail values are as follows: Grand Prize — A brand-new Ford Explorer 4×4 plus a trip for two (2) to Hawaii, including round-trip air transportation, six (6) nights hotel accommodation, a $1,400 meal/spending money stipend and $2,000 cash toward a new fashion wardrobe (approximate value: $28,000) or $15,000 cash; two (2) Second Prizes — A trip to Hawaii, including round-trip air transportation, six (6) nights hotel accommodation, a $1,400 meal/spending money stipend and $2,000 cash toward a new fashion wardrobe (approximate value: $11,000) or $5,000 cash; three (3) Third Prizes — $2,000 cash toward a new fashion wardrobe. All prizes are valued in U.S. currency. Travel award air transportation is from the commercial airport nearest winner's home. Travel is subject to space and accommodation availability, and must be completed by June 30, 1993. Sweepstakes offer is open to residents of the U.S. and Canada who are 21 years of age or older as of December 31, 1991, except residents of Puerto Rico, employees and immediate family members of Torstar Corp., its affiliates, subsidiaries, and all agencies, entities and persons connected with the use, marketing, or conduct of this sweepstakes. All federal, state, provincial, municipal and local laws apply. Offer void wherever prohibited by law. Taxes and/or duties, applicable registration and licensing fees, are the sole responsibility of the winners. Any litigation within the province of Quebec respecting the conduct and awarding of a prize may be submitted to the Régie des loteries et courses du Québec. All prizes will be awarded; winners will be notified by mail. No substitution of prizes is permitted.

4. Potential winners must sign and return any required Affidavit of Eligibility/Release of Liability within 30 days of notification. In the event of noncompliance within this time period, the prize may be awarded to an alternate winner. Any prize or prize notification returned as undeliverable may result in the awarding of that prize to an alternate winner. By acceptance of their prize, winners consent to use of their names, photographs or their likenesses for purposes of advertising, trade and promotion on behalf of Torstar Corp. without further compensation. Canadian winners must correctly answer a time-limited arithmetical question in order to be awarded a prize.

5. For a list of winners (available after 3/31/92), send a separate stamped, self-addressed envelope to: Silhouette Fashion A Whole New You Sweepstakes, P.O. Box 4665, Blair, NE 68009.

PREMIUM OFFER TERMS

To receive your gift, complete the Offer Certificate according to directions. Be certain to enclose the required number of "Fashion A Whole New You" proofs of product purchase (which are found on the last page of every specially marked "Fashion A Whole New You" Silhouette or Harlequin romance novel). Requests must be received no later than December 31, 1991. Limit: four (4) gifts per name, family, group, organization or address. Items depicted are for illustrative purposes only and may not be exactly as shown. Please allow 6 to 8 weeks for receipt of order. Offer good while quantities of gifts last. In the event an ordered gift is no longer available, you will receive a free, previously unpublished Silhouette or Harlequin book for every proof of purchase you have submitted with your request, plus a refund of the postage and handling charge you have included. Offer good in the U.S. and Canada only.

SLFW - SWPR

SILHOUETTE® OFFICIAL SWEEPSTAKES ENTRY FORM

4-FWSES-4

Complete and return this Entry Form immediately – the more entries you submit, the better your chances of winning!

- Entries must be received by **December 31, 1991.**
- A Random draw will take place on **January 30, 1992.**
- No purchase necessary.

Yes, I want to win a FASHION A WHOLE NEW YOU Sensuous and Adventurous prize from Silhouette:

Name _____ Telephone _____ Age _____

Address _____

City _____ State _____ Zip _____

Return Entries to: **Silhouette FASHION A WHOLE NEW YOU,**
P.O. Box 9056, Buffalo, NY 14269-9056   © 1991 Harlequin Enterprises Limited

PREMIUM OFFER

To receive your free gift, send us the required number of proofs-of-purchase from any specially marked FASHION A WHOLE NEW YOU Silhouette or Harlequin Book with the Offer Certificate properly completed, plus a check or money order (do not send cash) to cover postage and handling payable to Silhouette FASHION A WHOLE NEW YOU Offer. We will send you the specified gift.

OFFER CERTIFICATE

Item	A. SENSUAL DESIGNER VANITY BOX COLLECTION (set of 4) (Suggested Retail Price $60.00)	B. ADVENTUROUS TRAVEL COSMETIC CASE SET (set of 3) (Suggested Retail Price $25.00)
# of proofs-of-purchase	18	12
Postage and Handling	$3.50	$2.95
Check one	☐	☐

Name _____

Address _____

City _____ State _____ Zip _____

Mail this certificate, designated number of proofs-of-purchase and check or money order for postage and handling to: **Silhouette FASHION A WHOLE NEW YOU Gift Offer,** P.O. Box 9057, Buffalo, NY 14269-9057. Requests must be received by December 31, 1991.

ONE PROOF-OF-PURCHASE

4-FWSEP-4

To collect your fabulous free gift you must include the necessary number of proofs-of-purchase with a properly completed Offer Certificate.

© 1991 Harlequin Enterprises Limited

See previous page for details.